Falling Softly

Compass Girls, Book 4

Jayne Rylon and Mari Carr

Falling Softly

Copyright 2017 by Mari Carr

All Rights Reserved.

No part of this book, with the exception of brief quotations for book reviews or critical articles, may be reproduced or transmitted in any form or by any means, electronic or mechanical, including photocopying, recording, or by any information storage and retrieval system without express written permission from the author.

This is a work of fiction. Names, characters, places, and incidents are the product of the author's imagination or are used fictitiously, and any resemblance to actual persons, living or dead, business establishments, events, or locales is entirely coincidental.

ISBN: 978-1-941785-51-5

Editor: Amy Sherwood

Cover Artist: Jayne Rylon

Print Formatting: Mari Carr

Compass Girls, Book 4

Darkness has crept into Sterling Compton's charmed life, relentlessly stealing what's left of her grandmother's memories. When she happens upon a compelling stranger leaning against a broken-down pickup in the middle of nowhere, grief and a gut-deep attraction spur her to take that too-safe life by the horns.

From the instant Sterling emerges from her Jeep, Viho is drawn to her carefree spirit. Her innocent offer of a ride turns into the ride of his life in his truck bed—and he forgets why he meant to avoid Compton Pass at all costs.

He should have known that karma was waiting to laugh in his face. Especially when Viho figures out Sterling's father is the one who stood between him and the man *he* should have called "father."

Yet it's tough to hate someone who offers him a job. Especially when he and Sterling realize there's a living tie on the way that will bind Viho to her family forever—if he can convince her she's much more to him than an obligation.

Warning: Sometimes it's hard to let go, but every story has an ending. This one has a Native American hero with a chip on his shoulder the size of Wyoming and a vulnerable heroine who has a gift for polishing up diamonds in the rough. Some scenes may tug heartstrings so hard it'll hurt, but the oh-my-god orgasms make up for it.

Falling Softly

For all good things that have come to an end.

Prologue

Sterling Compton accepted a large, flat box from her father, Sam. She unraveled the lilac ribbon, then shredded the holographic wrapping paper beneath as the rest of her mega-extended family smiled from the other side of the kitchen table she—and her cousins, the Compass Girls—huddled around. Her grandmother, Vivi, laughed as the telltale rattle gave away the contents before Sterling could actually see the beads making the racket against the hard plastic organizer she revealed.

If the size of her smile could be measured by the ache in her cheeks, it might be setting a record for her sixteen years on Earth. And that was saying something. Her life had been full of joy. How could it not be, with a group of three cousins who were like her sisters, along with their younger brothers, the Compass Boys?

They had the entire Compass Ranch to roam on horseback. Plenty of places to play. So much love and fun she hadn't realized that not everyone was surrounded by sunshine that bright and warm. Only recently had she started to notice shadows on the fringes of her happy world.

Like when she'd met the boy at school who'd had no money for lunch. Vivi had listened to her story and gave her double the whole next week so he didn't have to sit in the corner with his arms wrapped around his middle.

Or when she'd seen a woman crying in the parking lot of the hospital when she'd gone along with Hope to visit Aunt Lucy one day. The way the woman had fingered a snipped plastic medical bracelet as she sobbed had sent chills up Sterling's spine.

Just last week she'd accidentally interrupted her dad having a teleconference with a supplier who'd tried to cheat the ranch. She'd never seen him angry before, but the curses he'd shouted at the man on the other side of the screen had made her eyes bulge.

For one moment, she paused, glancing around the familiar faces that had surrounded her. Protected her, for all of her life. Beyond them, the sun had nearly set outside and darkness crept in. She nibbled on the corner of her lip, tasting the sweetness of Vivi's cake there.

"Don't you like it?" Jade asked, earning an elbow in the ribs from Sienna.

"I do. It's great." Quick to correct them, Sterling refocused on the package in her hands and the bliss overflowing their home. A gift more precious than she could have dreamed to ask for.

If this is what it meant to *mature*, she wasn't sure she was onboard for that nonsense.

But presents, she could handle those.

Sterling jiggled the case in her hands, watching the light bounce off the multicolored glass. So pretty. So many colors, so many ways to arrange them. She couldn't wait to get started. Suddenly, choosing to celebrate her Sweet Sixteen with an epic craft session between just her, Hope, Sienna and Jade seemed like the best idea she'd ever had.

She glanced up at her mom and smiled, though the woman was too intuitive to be fooled so easily. A raised brow met her grin. Sterling explained, "There are so many possibilities. It's kind of…overwhelming."

Swallowing hard, she blinked back unexpected tears. Her mom smiled warmly and nodded as if, like always, she understood completely.

"If you work hard, you'll make something great of whatever you're given." Jake, one of the ranch hands, added another present to the one Sterling didn't want to let go of even for a second. A pair of jeweler's pliers. How like him to give her tools. She appreciated his useful gift. Of all of the ranch family, maybe his gruffness was preparing them for the road ahead more than she realized.

"Thank you," she said, and meant it.

Her dad clapped the guy on the back and they shared a secret smile. Jake was like her fourth uncle. The rest of the Compass Brothers and their wives contributed to her pile until she had everything she needed for the hobby she had shown some skill in at summer camp earlier this year. Gear, wire, clasps, art supplies for designing, stones and even a gem polisher. Everything she'd not-so-secretly longed for lay at her fingertips.

Embarrassed, she realized she'd talked for months now about the love she'd discovered for making jewelry. To say she'd been obsessed would be an understatement. Online video tutorials had occupied a lot of her summer hours, and she felt she had a lot of knowledge but hardly any experience. Time to change that.

She couldn't wait.

"Yes, we listen to you, honey." Vivi beamed as she handed over her present. She continued talking as Sterling unwrapped an assortment of gorgeous charms. "Passion makes any project perfect. You should follow your heart. Make something beautiful out of this gift you have and share it with others."

"I will," she promised.

With that, the crowd dispersed. Most of the male family members swarmed the cake for a second helping. Roughhousing and playfulness replaced the quiet intensity of the fleeting moment when she'd truly felt like an almost-adult for the first time. Thank goodness.

Sterling glanced around at her cousins, who inspected her bounty as they got ready to settle in for the crafting bonanza sleepover she'd opted for as her special Compass Girls celebration. As she gazed on the various components before her, she had an idea.

"You know, I bet we could make some necklaces to match school colors and sell them at the basketball games coming up." Sterling could already picture a neat design with alternating colors. She took out a length of wire and then snipped one for each of the other girls.

For a while, she was lost in her imagination, visualizing what could become of the metal and glass if she twisted here and pinched there. Like that. She hadn't realized the majority of her relatives had wandered off, either out to the barn or to their own homes, until one of the girls broke the silence.

"I'm sure *you* could have something awesome by next week's match." Hope snorted, glancing between the creation taking shape in Sterling's palm and the junk Jade dangled from her fingertip.

Sterling laughed. "Good point."

Jade dropped the lame attempt onto the table, then chewed one of her black-painted nails. Around the digit, she mumbled, "Tell me again why we didn't sneak out to that party up by the lake? All the popular boys are going to be there. I heard Jimmy talked his older brother into buying them a keg. There's probably still time. Once the old people go to bed…"

"No way!" Hope glared at their more rebellious cousin. "I'm not getting in trouble that deep. Do you know what my dads would do to us if we got caught? Or Uncle Sawyer, if the cops get called?"

"Besides, what is it with you and drinking?" Sterling honestly wondered what the appeal was. "Ever since we snuck that tequila on Sienna's birthday, it seems like that's all you care about. You can have plenty of fun without getting hammered, you know?"

Sterling almost regretted her harsh tone when Jade went quiet, staring at the mangled wire in her hand as she tried to make something other than a mess from the supplies.

Soon enough, though, the mood passed, helped along by Hope and her ever-bubbly personality. "Come on, guys. It's Sterling's birthday and we're going to spend it her way. Maybe there will be another party next weekend. Who knows?"

"Yeah." Sienna jumped in to smooth things over. "We've got plenty of time to do what everyone wants. Pretty much forever. A hundred years at least, right?"

Something in Sterling's stomach felt funny as she wondered if that was true. What was wrong with her today?

This time when she met Jade's stare, they seemed to have more in common.

"How about I make you a necklace?" Sterling scooted her chair closer and dragged the onyx slices toward them both. "I bet you'd like something like this. Or maybe I could set one of those cameo brooches in a swirly silver oval and tie it up with some of this black satin ribbon?"

"That sounds pretty cool." Jade knocked her shoulder into Sterling's. "I wish I was good at something like this."

"You'll find your talent soon." Sterling smiled,

hoping it wasn't a lie.

Time flew as she transformed basic materials into something spectacular. At least to her, since it was her first real piece of jewelry. Jade seemed equally impressed when she peeked up from the movie the rest of the girls watched. It was probably the third one in the marathon they'd kicked off after Sterling became completely engrossed in her project.

Modeling the results of Sterling's work, Jade intimidated them with her stark beauty, even if she seemed blind to it. They all jumped when someone's cell phone rang from the other side of the cottage. Her dad's.

No one called him this late.

He answered quickly, then listened. "Oh shit!" he barked. A few terse exchanges were followed by silence.

Something felt off. Hairs rose on Sterling's arm.

Curious, the girls crouched low as one. Holding hands, they snuck toward Sterling's mom and dad's room as quietly as a gaggle of teenagers could manage. It must have been awful if Sam and Cindi didn't notice the racket.

As the Compass Girls hovered near the cracked door, they overheard every whispered word of the conversation that followed. "It's bad, Cin. Antonio and Charlotte's girl, the one in Sterling's class…"

"Suzanne?" Cindi's voice held an edge Sterling couldn't remember hearing before. "What about her?"

"There's been an accident. A terrible one. Sawyer's at the scene. He was the first responder." Sam crossed the room. Through the gap, they watched him hug Cindi to his chest while she covered her face with her palms.

Her mom asked the question Sterling wanted to know the answer to herself. "Is Suzanne—"

"She's alive. Barely. Even if she makes it through the night…she's never going to be the same, though. Head injury. Brain trauma. Stuff like that." Sam cursed violently, demonstrating his expertise with the dirty words Sterling had just found out her dad knew how to use shockingly well. "Stupid kids. They were up at the lake drinking. Then attempted the drive home, shiny new licenses and all. You know that bad curve, near the Fuller's farm? They didn't make it. Hit a tree, then flipped down the embankment."

"How can we help?" Cindi wondered.

"Sawyer wanted to know if we could watch their boy tonight." Sam's voice sounded strained. "No kid should have to see this. Antonio and Charlotte are wrecked. Can't hardly think for themselves, never mind take care of Billy."

Sterling whipped her stare to the rest of her cousins, who seemed pale enough to glow in the dark. They all gawked at Jade. What if they'd gone too? It could easily have been them instead of Suzanne lying broken on the gravel road.

Gasping for air, Sterling considered the ripples one girl's foolish choices would have on the rest of her life. On her family. Sterling's brother, Bryant, and Billy were best friends. Would Billy realize this wasn't some impromptu sleepover when Sam picked him up from the sitter instead of his parents coming home from their night out?

Would the adults hide the bad stuff from the poor kid? How long could they keep it secret? Soon enough the truth had to come out. And when it did, Billy would be crushed.

The girls scrambled into the living room when Sam tugged on his jeans.

They collapsed, shell shocked, onto the couch. Still holding hands.

"This is my new lucky necklace." Jade lifted her fingers to run compulsively over the pendant Sterling had slaved over.

It was the first time in Sterling's life she clearly witnessed the raw ugliness of life behind the force field of sunshine and rainbows her family had constructed, recognizing darkness for what it truly was. Though it wouldn't be the last.

Because once the illusion had truly shattered, she couldn't recreate the paradise she'd thought she lived in.

Just like finding out there was no Santa, except a hundred times worse. Disappointment and a fear of loss were born into her world, never to leave. Ugly presents she hadn't asked for and couldn't return. Maybe their hundred years orbiting the sun was grossly overestimated.

Happy birthday, baby.

Chapter One

"No, Vivi. It's this way." Sterling Compton winced as she steered her grandmother, in super slow motion, toward the specialist's office for the unscheduled consultation he'd requested. Okay, so the convoluted path through the bowels of Compton Pass's hospital would put a snarled mess of jeweler's wire to shame. Still, they'd been this way a bajillion times in the past year for routine appointments. Her grandmother should know the route by heart.

Had never faltered before.

It wasn't that today was a particularly bad one for the woman either. She suffered from Alzheimer's. It'd been a while since she'd had terrific day, come to think of it. Lately, Sterling considered herself and the rest of her Compass Girl cousins lucky if Vivi remembered their names and didn't mix them up with their mothers. Hell, sometimes she would trade a mistaken identity for the days Vivi didn't respond at all, lost in her own thoughts.

Acid churned in Sterling's guts as she dreaded the final steep slope of her grandmother's decline. Day after day of seeing her like this had started to erode some of the impressions Sterling held dear of the strong, confident, independent woman her grandmother had always been. It frightened her to think that true person would be erased from her memory, replaced by this specter of her grandmother, in jeopardy of surrendering the most important thing she'd ever owned—her dignity. Maybe it would be better to be clueless. Maybe Vivi wasn't the one getting served the biggest shit sandwich in this deal.

Feeling sorry for herself wouldn't make Sterling's helping any more palatable. She tried to enjoy her time with her grandmother, while she still could.

"That's a pretty bracelet." Vivi twirled the silver cuff on Sterling's wrist, then winked. "Where'd you get it? My birthday is coming up soon, you know."

Taking a long, deep breath, Sterling didn't bother to correct her grandmother, who'd celebrated her birthday in the spring. Instead, Sterling focused on the genuine admiration, taking the compliment to heart. After all, it wasn't as if her grandmother was stroking her ego when she couldn't remember that jewelry was Sterling's business. Hanging around Vivi had conditioned her to live in the moment. "I made this. It's part of my new line for the store. Here, try it on."

She slipped the skin-warmed metal over her hand and threaded Vivi's gnarled fingers through the opening. It bobbled too far up Vivi's thin arm when the woman angled it for a better look. "Pretty. High-quality workmanship."

"Thanks." Sterling beamed.

"You made this?" Vivi asked, driving a white-hot poker into Sterling's heart. Though it cost her, she smiled and nodded.

"Almost there." She coached Vivi around one final bend, then considered arranging a wheelchair for their next visit as she lowered her grandmother into a plastic bucket chair outside the specialist's office. The woman closed her eyes for a second or two as she settled gingerly into the seat and rubbed her knee.

They'd hardly been there long enough for Vivi to wonder where she'd gotten her new bracelet from a handful of times when Dr. Martin popped his head out. "Mrs. Compton. So nice to see you today."

"Dr. Phillips?" Vivi seemed shocked. As she should, since poor Doc had passed away at least a decade ago. He'd been the man who'd treated Sterling's grandfather, JD, before she'd been born.

"No, ma'am. I'm Dr. Martin." A somber mask gradually replaced the initial welcoming optimism that had brightened his face. Both he and Sterling knew where this was headed. "Would you mind waiting out here a moment while I speak with your granddaughter? If you need anything, my assistant, Claudine, is right down there."

"Of course not." Vivi smiled as she peeked over to the nearby desk the doctor pointed toward. "I think we've got some time before our volunteer shift begins. Honey, if he wants your number, I'd recommend giving it to him."

Vivi hadn't spent her days cheering up patients in a very long time. Neither Sterling nor the doctor planned on mentioning that, though. And if they weren't going to burst her bubble about the purpose of her trip, they certainly weren't about to remind her that she'd met Dr. Martin's lovely wife on many occasions.

Boot heels clacked ominously in the thick silence as Dr. Martin ushered Sterling into an exam room and shut the door quietly behind him. "Look, Sterling, I feel like I've gotten to know you well enough to guess you'd like me to cut the bullshit and tell things to you straight, right?"

"Of course. No need for a charming bedside manner with me, Doc." She crossed her arms, hugging herself as if she could prevent his words from piercing her chest like a fiery arrow.

"Right." He grimaced. "The trial isn't working for your grandmother. It's clear now that we're not doing any good. In fact, we are probably doing harm in the grand scheme of things."

"What?" Sterling tipped her head to one side.

"The medicine your grandmother is receiving is very limited. By continuing her participation, we're denying a candidate who might respond well to the treatment a chance at a normal life." He sighed and reached for Sterling's hand, but she shrugged, angling away. "I'm sorry, Sterling."

"What will happen if we cut her off? Will she get worse even faster?" Freezing fingers of dread reached into Sterling's gut at the thought. Her legs shook and she locked her knees to keep from wobbling. The day was coming. They knew it was. But she wasn't ready to say goodbye yet.

Why hadn't she accepted her dad's offer to accompany them today? She could really use his broad shoulders to lean on right now. Except this was going to be even harder for him to hear about his own mother. Shit.

"It's hard to tell. We can't say for sure if the drug has been ineffective or if it has successfully slowed her decline considering she has one of the most severe cases I've seen in years." He paused.

"Don't stop now. Spit it out." Sterling eyed the doc as he paced before her.

"Observing how Vivi reacts once we discontinue the medication could be valuable data for the study. We could draw conclusions about whether the decline is more marked—"

"Wait." Sterling shook her head even as her fists balled. "Are you telling me that you want to experiment on my grandmother? Yank her drugs to see what happens? She could die!"

Catching her breath took conscious effort. So did beating back the waves of blackness assaulting her.

"Sterling, the truth is we've been researching all along. You know that." He held his hands up, palms out. "I know this is hard. But talk it over with your family. Try to think logically instead of emotionally. Our board of directors has only continued her enrollment in the program this long because of your family's generosity to this institution. I personally don't believe that Mrs. Compton would approve if she knew the truth. If she was capable of logic..."

Guilt slammed through Sterling as she realized how selfish she was being. All of them were. Prolonging Vivi's suffering for their own comfort at the expense of another family... Well, that wasn't how they were raised.

Damn straight. If Vivi understood the ramifications, she'd pull the plug herself.

Probably would have months ago.

"O-okay." She had to clear her throat to agree. "Give me tonight to round everyone up for a family meeting."

Dr. Martin nodded. "I'm so sorry, Sterling. Truly, I am."

And why did she feel like she'd be hearing that a lot?

"Thanks." She scrubbed her fingers over her face and prepared to paste on a smile for Vivi. They had to be strong for her now, like she'd always been for them. After losing the love of her life, she'd carried on and shepherded the extended family that had provided Sterling with everything she could have hoped for. Now it was her turn to live up to that legacy.

Even while her heart shattered.

Sterling knuckled moisture from the corners of her eyes, squared her shoulders and yanked open the door. One problem. The seat where Vivi had waited for her was empty.

"Oh crap." Sterling peeked down the hall in either direction, praying her grandmother had spotted someone familiar and gone to say hello. Or maybe gone to chat with Claudine. No such luck. The woman was on the phone while two other people hovered in front of her, blocking her view of the waiting area.

"What's—?" Dr. Martin caught on quick when he peeked over her shoulder and caught her frantically sweeping the unnaturally bright-white interior for any hint of her grandmother. "I'll call the front desk. They won't let her leave without you."

"Right." Sterling didn't wait for him to put their safety net in place. She jogged down the hall, peeking into every room that she passed. Including one that held a half-dressed man prepping for some surely stressful test.

"Sorry, sorry!" Shutting the door as quickly as possible, she trotted along until she came to the next intersection. For a little old lady, Vivi seemed to have sprouted wings. She couldn't have gotten far.

Reading the screen hung on the wall, Sterling couldn't decide which way to turn. Until she spotted, "Long-term Residential Care". *Please, please.* That had to be it. She went with her gut.

Picking up steam, she caught nasty glares from the nurses and even a shout to slow down from an orderly as she sprinted past, still craning her neck wildly in every direction without a glimpse of her grandmother.

After crashing into the corner of a cart, a direct hit to her hipbone, Sterling slowed. Her heart raced and her breath sawed in and out of her lungs as she approached the open glass doors that lead into a different section of the hospital.

Linoleum gave way to hardwood floors, and walls covered with bookshelves sat opposite the receptionist. Beyond the woman with thick-rimmed glasses staring curiously at her was a large, open area full of plants and couches and low tables brimming with puzzles. Natural light nearly made the whole place glow.

Sterling squinted against the glare, which couldn't disguise this place for the prison it truly was. Designed to house patients who required full-time assistance, there'd always been something about the serene surroundings that had made her skin crawl. It was as if the designers had been trying to stifle an uprising.

Vivi had brought her here a few days a week for nearly a decade. They'd volunteered, playing board games and generally trying to keep people company. One person more than the others, though.

"Everything okay, Sterling?" Jeanette, the receptionist, canted her head as she stared.

"Fine." She winced. "I think. Have you seen my grandmother?"

"Of course. Vicky is in the solarium with Suzanne. Just like the old days, huh?" The pitiful smile she flashed Sterling was reminiscent of the looks she'd seen people give some of the residents. Hopeless. False, though well intended. Reassuring in no way at all.

Thank God they'd talked Vivi out of her ludicrous plan to enter a facility not that different from this one. Sure, the staff gave the best care they could to the residents, but it just wasn't the same as living at home. Surrounded by family.

Vivi had lost so much already, she shouldn't have to surrender absolutely everything.

When Sterling raised an absentminded hand to acknowledge Jeanette then nearly stumbled into the dazzling space beyond, her breath caught in her lungs. Her eyes stung as she blinked rapidly. She wished she could say her reaction had to do with the flood of brilliance instead of the fact that Vivi could have easily been a patient, sitting on the cheery sofa, staring blankly at Suzanne, who stared blankly back.

Though none of them had ever said so out loud, they all knew that one or all of the Compass Girls could have been in her shoes. That horrible accident on Sterling's sixteenth birthday had stolen Suzanne's bright future. Unless you counted what the glistening skylights did to her hair, which had gone stark white following the crash.

Sterling doubled over. She clenched her gut and bit her lip to keep from crying out.

What had she done with her life to make the most of the gift it was?

Unlike her cousins, she didn't have someone special to share her time with. No one waited for her at home, in the cottage her cousins had rapidly grown out of. There wasn't anyone to share her evenings with. Her jewelry shop was the only thing she had to brag about. And even that hadn't really blossomed to the full potential she daydreamed about.

Not without taking her shop online. Expanding, though that would mean taking out a loan for more frontage. Reaching out to the world to share her talents with more than Compton Pass, Wyoming, or the regional vendors who sold her creations on consignment. All the things she'd been too afraid to do. Talents wasted away in her small-town showcase.

Maybe all this time she'd thought of Suzanne's tragedy, and Vivi's, she'd had everything mixed up. They'd had something valuable to lose.

Right then and there she promised herself she'd be bolder. Embrace her wild side, which she constantly suppressed. Take some damn chances and make her life *count*.

"You all right, hon?" A nurse Sterling didn't recognize put her hand in the small of Sterling's back. "You look like you're going to pass out. Why don't you have a seat?"

"I'm okay." A lie. "Haven't eaten yet today. I'll be fine."

That could be another untruth. She wasn't sure of anything anymore. Except that she planned to go forward differently than she'd been trudging on.

"Hi, Suz. I hope you don't mind—I came for Vivi." Sterling wrestled the panic inside her that threatened to overwhelm her sanity. When she turned toward Vivi, something brushed her fingers. Suzanne. Had she reached out intentionally or had it been a coincidence?

Sterling stared at her old friend, but no recognition dawned in her glassy eyes.

"Come on, Vivi. Shift's over. I'm going to take you home." She refocused on her grandmother.

"Already?" The woman snapped out of her daze as if they'd been chatting all along. "It seems like we just got here."

"Funny, I feel like I've been here forever." She sighed, then helped Vivi out of the plush couch.

They didn't talk the rest of the way out to the car even though they inched along the snarled corridors. Or even when Sterling nodded to the woman posted at the door, who let them pass without comment.

Sterling buckled her grandmother in, then rounded the hood to slide into the driver's seat as the woman twisted the bangle on her wrist, mesmerized by the hand-worked leaves. "Ready, Vivi?"

"Yep. It's almost time to start supper." She paused. "Do you know where I got this bracelet, Cindi?"

Sterling's eyes watered as she pretended it didn't hurt to be called her mother. For Vivi to have already forgotten her gift. Raw from the news and the scare and her revelations, she barely held her shit together. When she didn't answer, Vivi continued, "I think you'd better hold onto this until we find out who it belongs to."

Sterling figured it wasn't worth the hassle of the fifteen phone calls she'd get over the next few days from concerned family members, worried that Vivi had picked it up in a store and forgotten to pay for it. Swallowing hard, she took back the gift, slipped the bracelet onto her wrist, then drove toward Compass Ranch and the rest of her life beyond those fences.

Chapter Two

Sterling barely escaped the laser stare of her cousin, Hope, as she transferred her grandmother to the other young woman's care. Normally they'd sit and chat awhile, enjoying their time with Vivi. Brew some tea, share ranch gossip and cook dinner together so their grandmother didn't attempt to operate the stove without subtle supervision.

Not today.

With her obligation complete, Sterling needed to escape before she ensnared the rest of her family in the turmoil she'd already been exposed to after Dr. Martin's sentencing. Dramatic? Maybe, but that's how it felt.

Rolling the windows down, she let the wind whip her chestnut hair around her face. The tips lashed her and made her eyes water. At least, that was what she identified as the culprit when moisture trickled down her cheeks while she passed through town.

She bounced along in her retro Jeep, letting the rural scenery soothe her. Nature did that for her. It always had.

Blacktop transformed into gravel and tar. Shops became houses and then occasional farms. As the miles ticked by, plowed fields gave way to grasslands. They rolled off to where they met the mountains in the distance. Crystal clear water, which would be freezing if she parked and dipped her toes in, streamed beneath the old wooden bridge she rumbled across. In the distance, a trio of wild mustangs galloped.

Red rocks and scraggly silverberry bushes inspired a design. Finally, the perfect thing to do with those unusual garnets she'd had lying around popped into her mind. She searched the road ahead for a place to pull over so she could haul out her sketchbook to capture the flash of brilliance before it passed.

Except just then, she spotted the glint of sunlight off something distinctly not natural. A hunk of metal. As she crested a gentle hill and neared, she realized it was a busted truck. Way out here, miles from town, it would be irresponsible for her to leave without checking on its most likely stranded owner.

Slowing down, she approached the vehicle. From this distance, it was easy to detect the open hood and the wisps of blue smoke drifting from the engine of the rust bucket. Not a good sign.

But when she got closer still and noticed the man leaning against the clunker, she whistled.

Enormous, he reminded her of a sequoia. Earthy, strong and beautiful. Majestic. One glimpse at him had a thousand ideas sparking to life. Her pencil would be worn to a stub before she could draw them all.

His hair beat hers in both the intensity of its inky blackness and the thickness of its straight length. Classic Native American features made his face bold and strikingly handsome. But his relaxed pose, ankles crossed with arms up and back on either side of him—splayed across the top edge of the truck bed—had her swallowing hard.

Sterling squirmed in the driver's seat.

Despite his seeming casualness, his broad chest

puffed outward, making it clear he could take care of himself. Even if she'd been a two-hundred-and-fifty pound rancher in his prime, she'd have been no concern for this guy.

More sharply than she intended, Sterling hit the brakes, stirring up some dust as she bobbled onto the shoulder behind his vehicle. Instinctively, one of her hands flew to her phone, nestled in her wristlet. She peeked at its screen, double-checking the strength of her signal out here. Thank goodness for satellites.

Furiously, she swiped her finger across the device, sending her cousins a quick text. *I found a stray smoking hot man on the side of the road. Going to play the Good Samaritan. Probably give him a ride into town. If I don't text you back in an hour with details, he turned out to be a psychopath, has eaten me alive and is burying the leftovers in the wilderness. Send help.*

Three beeps pinged off the inside of her vehicle almost immediately.

Be careful! From Hope.

Don't joke! From Sienna.

Hot, you say? Have fun. Jade, of course.

Gotta go. Sterling laughed softly to herself as she tucked her phone away. She'd probably pay for that later—with an epic pillow fight, or having to muck out stalls with Jade, or by baking dessert for the other Compass Girls—but she didn't care at the moment.

Still amused, she glanced up and caught her sexy stranger staring at her. He hadn't moved a single muscle. Not even a twitch. As if afraid of spooking her, he waited for her to approach. His carefully constructed docile illusion didn't fool her for a nanosecond.

Dangerous though he might be, his raw sensuality drew her. She gazed right back at him, noting the rich chocolate of his eyes and the faint scar decorating the corner of his mouth. Cataloging every detail of his flawless imperfection, she clutched the steering wheel with both hands.

He seemed sort of familiar and yet unlike anyone she'd ever known. So much *more*.

She swore she could read a million thoughts in his stare during the span of a single heartbeat. What the hell?

And then he smiled.

It seemed a tiny bit contrived, and not as reassuring as he probably intended. Like a Big Bad Wolf whose grin only showed off his fangs. Yet, it might have been the most gorgeous thing she'd seen in a year. Considering the gems surrounding her day in and day out, that was saying something.

Her fingers trembled as they opened her door.

When she slid out of the Jeep, her boots weren't as steady on the ground as she would have expected....preferred, really.

It must have been the trip to the hospital throwing her off her game.

Sterling had halved the distance between them, coming to stand with her feet apart and her thumbs hooked in the pockets of her denim skirt, before either of them spoke. She broke the silence. "Truck crapped out on you, huh?"

"Yep." He still didn't budge. As if that might make her less aware of the fact that he could overpower her in a hurry, if he was so inclined.

"Waiting for roadside assistance?" She wondered why he was so calm. Most people, even seasoned ranch hands, would be leery about spending the night so far out of touch from town. Without proper supplies, it wouldn't be very comfortable at best and could be dangerous if the person stranded didn't have at least moderate survival skills. Already the air grew brisk enough that she resisted the temptation to hug herself.

"Nah. Don't have a cell." He shrugged, the motion only highlighting the ripped shoulders beneath his thin T-shirt and the chiseled sinew of his forearms.

Who didn't carry a phone these days? Maybe he couldn't afford one, if his truck and ripped jeans were anything to guess by.

"So you're just going to chill out here and hope for someone to pass by?" She arched a brow at his nonchalance.

"Seems to be a solid plan so far." This time his grin seemed genuine. "I didn't expect my rescue squad to be quite so pretty, though. Lucky me."

Bright white teeth flashed from behind his smile. It hit her in the gut, knocking the wind from her as if she'd fallen off one of the ranch horses. Full lips curved upward and his eyes danced with reflected light. She'd only seen eyes so vibrant, with flecks of gold, like that on one other person in her life.

He could have been the very definition of *alive*. The something elusive she'd been craving after this afternoon's bleak reminder of her mortality.

Life's irony gripped her, and she laughed. At her acquaintance's wit and flirting, some. But mostly at the pure exhilaration caused by riding the rollercoaster of her existence. Peaks and valleys. Everyone went through them, clinging desperately to the safety rails and trying not to piss their pants on the plunge down, then enjoying the view when things were looking up, she supposed.

Beaming, she planned to make the most of this sudden peak.

Then it was his turn to be rendered speechless. His eyes widened and his pupils dilated as he soaked in her joy and amusement. Fingers gripped the edge of the truck tighter, as if he might give up his charade and finally approach her if he didn't cling to the metal.

Maybe even go crazy and shake her hand. Who knew?

Something warned Sterling that if they touched, even with that itty-bit of skin on skin, sparks would fly and risk kindling a blaze that would set the entire early-fall landscape on fire.

So she dodged. She jutted her chin toward the wrench lying abandoned on the tailgate of his truck and the greasy rag beside it. "So I guess you couldn't get her going again, huh? I could take a look. I'm pretty good with machines and stuff like that. Working with my hands."

In fact, her father's best friend, Jake, had helped her rebuild her entire Jeep from junk. The model from late last century suited her perfectly, classic and funky all at once.

"I'm pretty sure it's not fixable." He grimaced. "But you're welcome to poke around if it'll make you feel useful."

"Sure thing. I'm Sterling, by the way." She snatched up the tool and passed within reach of the gentle giant, who smiled softly at her. "If I can't do anything with it either, I'll be glad to give you a ride into town or call a tow truck for you. You know, since you're so scared of me that you can't move, never mind get in my car."

He chuckled, low and half as rusty as his pick-up. When she peeked up at him from beneath his hood, he seemed startled, as if humor hadn't played a big part in his life so far. Maybe it hadn't. He sure looked like a hard man. One she'd love to tame. A challenge the cocky young guns on the ranch and in town didn't pose for her.

Right then she vowed to help him turn around what had to be a shitty day, a perfect match for hers.

When he finally caved and pushed off the truck, ambling to her side, she held her breath. His shadow fell across her, blocking out the sun entirely. Clearly, he'd been slouching. Probably a smart move, though she wasn't the sort of woman to cow easily.

Putting out one hand, he said, "Viho."

"Interesting name." She shook it, marveling at how he swallowed her fingers with heat and a gentle pressure that didn't crush her but didn't treat her like she was delicate filigree either.

"I could say the same." He flashed her another semi-smile. "Mine's Native American. It means Chief."

"Seriously?" Sterling nodded, impressed. "So are you royalty or something?"

He certainly had an air of nobility about him, despite his commoner's clothes.

"Nah." He shook his head a bit. "I guess I could have been. If we still had chiefs, my grandfather would have been it. The small reservation I grew up on looked to him for approval. But getting involved in our government wasn't my path. Causing a rift in our community was never my intention. And besides, I'm nobody's leader."

"How did you know that?" she wondered. After today, she was starting to doubt herself and her life choices where she never had before.

At first, she didn't think he intended to answer. She figured that was a pretty personal thing to ask a guy you'd spoken fewer words to than you'd say to a drive-thru attendant in the course of ordering a meal. But something about him made her feel as if they'd known each other for a hell of a lot longer than three point two seconds. Maybe it was the way he didn't pressure her, letting her take the lead in their interactions and conversation, unlike most guys she met, who were eager to pinpoint anything they had in common. Some way to get closer to her, either because they were interested in moving up the ranks at Compass Ranch or because they wanted in her pants. Or both. Kill two birds with one cock, so they seemed to think.

Instead, Viho reminded her of Jake, widely recognized as the best man around for taming wild horses. He had that same aloof patience that lured in the wild beasts and made them believe they were safe. And they were. Jake lived up to that implied promise. He cared for all his creatures, went above and beyond to see that they had everything he could give them.

It also could have been the sadness she sensed lurking behind Viho's spectacular eyes that struck a chord.

"First, the place I grew up wasn't the norm. It was culturally conservative. Dominated by a few extremist families that would never have seen past my less-than-pure blood. I'd have spent my entire life outvoted by the rest of the council regardless of how worthy my ideas were of their support. We'd have wasted everyone's time in one giant pissing match, no one moving forward. It's probably cowardly, but getting more involved seemed like a waste of time. Turning that tide was impossible. It never sat right on me anyway. Politics. People shouting over each other instead of understanding the other's point of view. I've always enjoyed being outside, alone, listening to nature…"

No wonder he hadn't been worried about spending the night outdoors.

"What does it tell you?" she asked.

And he shut down as surely as if she'd called him a loser.

"Hey." She paused her examination to lay a hand on his wrist. They both shivered in response. His skin was balmy against hers and his pulse jumped beneath the pads of her fingers at the contact. "I wasn't fucking around. Not making fun of you. I was serious."

"Oh." He sighed. Suddenly he seemed to age, and Sterling realized he was significantly older than she'd first thought. Maybe thirty-five or forty to her twenty-four. A man with some experience didn't sound like such a bad thing to her. Hopefully, she hadn't come off as some punk kid harassing him. "I guess I should have said that when it's quiet around me I can hear myself think. And I don't feel as out of place in the universe. If I stop listening too long, I start to feel like I don't belong here and never have. And that's totally a strange thing to admit. To anyone. But especially to…you know, you."

He scrunched his eyes closed and pinched the bridge of his nose.

"I guess that means we've passed that awkward introductory stage of our relationship." With that lame attempt at a joke, she released him and tried to concentrate. On his words. On the truck. On anything but putting her hands on him again. Maybe sliding her palms beneath his shirt to steal some of his warmth and map the contours of his prime body.

Because suddenly, she really wanted to show him that he was in the exact right place in the cosmos, and so was she.

"It's kind of weird, you know. I've always thought I knew where I was meant to be. But lately, things are changing, and I think that might be worse. Finding out that how you thought things were supposed to be isn't going to last forever, and that your life is your family's, not your own."

"I know *exactly* what you mean, Sterling." He gazed at her with such intensity that she had to clear her throat and deliberately turn away. "And when that anchor gets yanked up and you start to drift, it's easy to get dizzy. To lose your way."

"Is that how you ended up stranded on the side of

the road in the middle of nowhere?" She recalled the black, red and white bedroll she'd spotted in the bed of the truck. It looked like he'd used it. A lot. Not just for picturesque camping trips to manicured grounds, either.

"I suppose it was the start of that path." He shrugged, kicking a rock into the distance.

The grief radiating off him reminded her too much of what she'd been feeling when she left Compass Ranch earlier—the pain she'd been trying to obliterate, if even for a few hours.

So she steered the conversation to less dangerous ground. Like the cooling weather.

Viho rewarded her change of subjects with the hint of a smile and the loosening of his tense shoulders. As they chitchatted, she tinkered with his engine. It quickly became clear that his assessment was accurate. The thing was toast.

Surrendering, she turned toward Viho at the same instant he leaned in for a closer look. They plastered together. Instinctively, her hands flew to his chest to brace herself. And she smeared grease all over his soft, charcoal cotton shirt.

"Son of a bitch." She tried to wipe a smudge off and only splattered it more. "I'm so sorry."

"No problem." His easygoing nature counterbalanced her impending freak-out, which would only enhance the social awkwardness that had always plagued her. But when he reached down, grabbed the hem of the tee and whipped it over his head, he struck her dumb.

Muscles rippled as he moved, hardness covered with smooth, tan skin she wished she had a right to touch. "Uh..."

"It was an accident. No harm." He wadded up the fabric and tossed it into the back of the truck.

Except there might be some damage to her heart

if it didn't start beating again where it'd nearly exploded in her ribcage. It was time for her to admit it. She had never drooled over a man, not even a movie star or that guy she'd exchanged some heated emails with through an online matchmaking site, the way she lusted after Viho. Instant and vicious, attraction seethed between them.

"Sterling," he murmured.

"Yeah?"

"I think we'd better wrap up here so you can take me into town now."

"What if I don't really want to do that anymore?" She couldn't stop herself from being honest when he'd been so open with her earlier.

"Then I'll wait for the next person to come by." He shrugged, but she didn't miss the flash of disappointment in his warm stare.

Did he think so little of himself that he didn't understand her implication?

"Viho, this is not the time to be dense." Brave, sure, she could be. But making the first move in this situation… Well, that was a little outrageous, even for her.

"What's that supposed to mean?" He encroached on her personal space then, and she loved it.

"I think I'd rather stay here with you and listen to what nature is telling *me* right now." She wiped her hand on her skirt, then reached up to his cheek.

"You can't mean that." His eyes went wide. "Are you for real? Maybe I didn't drink enough water today. I've been stuck out here for a while."

Sterling smiled. She knew she was doing the right thing. He'd needed to find her as much as she'd needed to discover him today. For whatever reason, they were here in the same place at the same time. Wasting that opportunity—divine or pure dumb luck—would not be wise.

Sterling might not have believed in fate before, but she could be converted.

"Does this seem like I mean it?" She launched herself at Viho then, sure he wouldn't allow her to fall. Wrapping her arms around his neck, she went onto her tiptoes.

He didn't leave her straining for long. His broad hands cupped the back of her thighs and lifted her to his level. The tips of her boots dangled off the ground as their bodies aligned. Locking them tighter, she wrapped her legs around his hips and crossed her ankles even as her hands rested on either side of his neck. A breeze cooled her ass when her skirt rode up due to her very unladylike position.

Holding her as if she was as dainty as her cousin, Hope, he stared into her eyes until she lunged forward, plastering her lips on his before he could bring either one of them to their senses. That was when his gentlemanly exterior sheared away.

Viho growled as he kissed her, walking forward until her back knocked into the truck near where he'd stood when she'd first spied him. Her front molded to his bare chest and her greedy fingers explored his neck then his thick hair. As much of his muscular shoulders as she could reach.

If her nails scoring his heated flesh bothered him, he didn't show it. Instead, he devoured her mouth like a drowning man who'd been offered one last gasp of fresh air. It was delicious. The taste of him, vanilla and spice. Addictive bliss whited out everything wrong with her world and highlighted each pleasurable sensation that rushed in to take its place. The world glowed as if their passion electrified everything around them.

Sterling sighed, melting into Viho when his tongue caressed hers, just the way she liked. A shockwave of delight burst from her core, spreading outward in a flash of tingles to all of her extremities. The buzzing amplified when Viho turned up the heat, his hands sliding to her ass and squeezing.

He held her tight to him while he ravaged her mouth. His hips pressed forward, imprinting the long bulge of his hard-on into the softness of her mound.

A delighted whimper escaped her parted lips. Immediately, he froze.

"No, no," she urged in a husky whisper. "That was a good sound. Don't stop now."

"This is insane." He grunted softly when he rocked against her again as if he couldn't help himself. "We shouldn't."

"I don't care." Sterling nuzzled his neck, letting her teeth rake the sensitive spot below his jaw.

"Not now, you don't. But will you later?" Viho rested his forehead on hers. "I don't want you to have any regrets."

"I'll only be sorry if we don't live in the moment. We're here, together, right now and I don't want to waste a bit of whatever the hell this attraction is." Begging wasn't her style, but she was about to do it anyway. "Unless you have a girlfriend or something?"

"No." He breathed hard, as if trying to regain control.

And she was having none of that.

"Funny," she murmured as she nibbled his lip, intent on seduction.

"Hmm?" He didn't seem that interested in her musings as he detoured from his arguments to kiss her in return.

"Today doesn't seem so chilly anymore."

His answering laugh rumbled through his chest.

Sterling swore she could feel the echo straight through to her heart. Inspired, she toed off one boot and then the other, hoping the sound of the leather hitting the ground would trigger an avalanche of clothes joining them.

"You're sure?" he doubled-checked.

"Less talking, Viho. More kissing. Lots more." She purred as she rippled against his torso, making him pant using the body wave she and her Compass cousins had practiced while learning to dirty dance in their living room.

"Right. You know that old saying, never look a gift horse in the mouth—"

"Are you calling me a horse?" She quirked a brow at him.

"Don't hate me later, okay? And, hey, I love horses." His crooked grin curled one corner of his sinful lips.

"Well, in that case…"

Viho laughed softly. He cupped her face in his palms, then kissed her with more tenderness and less hunger this time. "I don't know where the hell you came from, girl, but I'm glad our paths crossed today."

"Me too," Sterling walked her fingers down his rock-solid pecs. "Now make it an afternoon I'll never forget, okay?"

"I'll try my best." He groaned when she spread her legs wider around him, inviting him closer, until neither of them could deny the thick ridge of his cock pressing at the damp lace of her panties. He kissed her neck, making her sigh and press into his hold even as he leaned his shoulders into her harder.

Pinned between his smoldering body and the cool steel of the vehicle, she shuddered.

He took the hint, reaching between them to yank open the fly of his jeans.

With a groan, he released his erection, drawing it through the opening of the well-worn denim. Sterling didn't hesitate—she arched her back, seeking the blunt tip of his cock even though she couldn't possibly align them on her own, especially not through the fabric of her underwear.

Damn it, why couldn't she be a superhero with the ability to disintegrate clothes?

Viho guided his cock to her, nudging aside her panties, eliminating the final barrier between them.

"Hang on." He paused.

"No. Don't stop." Okay, so it wasn't like she'd been waiting very long. But still, she was impatient to have him inside her, filling her with something other than the poisonous dread that had taken hold of her soul earlier. "I told you—"

"What day is it?" Viho gave her shoulders a small shake, enough to snap her back to reality. "Focus, Sterling. It's important."

"Thursday, I think." She racked her brain for a moment trying to remember something so mundane when he made her feel…extraordinary. "Why?"

"No, the date." He gritted his teeth. The muscle in his jaw flexed as he held himself separate from her.

"September 27th…no. It's the 28th."

"Shit, that's what I thought. Look…" He eased off her a bit, or would have if she hadn't wrapped her arms around his neck and dragged him back against her where his weight and heat felt so damn right. "I'm Vasalgeled. But my prescription expires at the end of the month. Damn thing's good for five years and it's going to run out any day. Just my shitty luck."

"To me it looks like today might have been perfect timing after all." Her lips curved into a wicked smile. "If we'd run into each other next week, then we'd have been screwed. I don't have any other protection with me. But I'm not about to sacrifice having you. Besides, isn't that like a sell-by date on a carton of milk?"

"I'm not sure." He shook his head as he tossed her a wry grin coupled with a pitiful stare.

"One of my cousins has been trying to start a family. They told her that her fiancés would have to be off their prescription for three months before she could realistically expect to get pregnant."

"Are you sure?" He broke eye contact and looked up at the sky as if begging someone to save him, or maybe to give him strength. "I'm not the kind of guy to take risks like that. Why don't we go into town, have something to eat, get to know each other—"

"If *you're* not sure…" She tried to hide her disappointment. Honorable and respectable. Great, she'd found a guy who checked all her boxes. Except today that wasn't what she was interested in having ticked.

"No. I want you. Make no mistake." His gaze returned to hers like a rubber band snapping into shape after being stretched. This time it was solid, unwavering. "It's just that I don't do things like this. Impulsive. Reckless."

"Me either." Sterling held her hands up. He took them and threaded their fingers together before placing them on either side of her head, capturing her completely. With his body supporting her, he stared down at her. She squeezed his fingers. "Any other day, I wouldn't even consider this. But today is different. This is what I want. *You* are exactly what I need right now."

"I don't think I've ever been what someone needed before." Bitterness tainted his baritone. "Don't expect me to turn away from a temptation as sweet as you, Sterling."

"I promise. That's the last thing I'm hoping for right now." She sighed when he relaxed into her, eliminating any distance between them.

The shift allowed her to sink onto him, his cock perfectly positioned to penetrate her moist folds.

Viho stared into her eyes. Both of them held their breath.

Until she whispered, "Do it."

And he complied.

Chapter Three

Viho freed one hand from Sterling's grasp momentarily to shove his jeans down his hips a bit and support the base of his shaft as the blunt head probed her opening. An involuntary gasp left her parted lips when his thickness breached her, stretching her around his welcome invasion.

A sharp, sudden intensity assaulted her.

He reacted immediately, stopping mid-motion. His cock pulsed as he controlled himself long enough to check in with her. "Too much?"

"Just need a second." She winked at him. "You're a big guy."

"Not all it's cracked up to be." He grimaced. "I'm not the kind of douchebag who enjoys hurting women."

Traveling lower with a string of kisses that started at her mouth and ended at her collarbones, he seemed like he might take his time about things. Opt for the scenic route. Ease his passage. Most days she'd appreciate his consideration. Not today.

"Not necessary."

"I want to taste you." Unapologetic, he stared into her eyes as he admitted it.

"How about you make a meal out of me to get me ready for round two?" She winced at how badly her body craved him inside her. "I need you. Now. It's fine. I'm good."

Sterling reached for his cock, attempting to insert him deeper within her aching body. Hovering on the cusp of something that promised to be glorious was killing her. Instead of letting her lead him around by the dick, he took charge.

"I can only hold back so much." He grunted as he slipped another inch inside her.

"Good." She would have teased him more, but it was impossible to concentrate as he lit up every nerve ending along her channel like the lights on a runway guiding a jumbo jet home. "Gah!"

It was about as coherent as she could manage when he impaled her on his cock.

Classy, nope. Sassy, definitely not. Honest…absolutely.

And he seemed to soak up her appreciation.

Viho cursed, then let go of her hands, allowing gravity to fully embed his thick shaft. Nature gifted them both with the resulting pleasure. She strangled his cock with the rings of muscle in her pussy, hugging him as he began to slide in and out of her the barest bit.

By bending his knees then wrapping one arm around her waist between her and the truck, he was able to fuck her with short, powerful jabs that ground their pelvises together, ensuring her clit rubbed against his body with every movement. Her hard nipples too.

When he returned his mouth to hers for intermittent kisses as they both gulped for air, she knew it wouldn't take long for her to come around him. She bit her lip as she concentrated, not on reaching orgasm but on holding it off so she could enjoy their primal meeting for as long as possible.

Viho ran his free hand up her ribs until he could wedge it between them and cup her breast. He thumbed the tip as he continued to plunge into her moist depths. Though her clothes muted the sensation, it was enough. Overloaded with rapture, Sterling's concentration broke. And as quickly as that, she shattered around Viho without warning.

Instead of triggering his orgasm, her pleasure only seemed to inspire him to rut hard against her, thrilling in the tug of her spasming flesh. "That's right. Come on my cock. Show me how much you like getting fucked by a stranger on the side of the road."

Oh, God. He was a dirty talker too? Sterling whipped her head from side to side as another burst of bliss prolonged, or maybe renewed, her climax. Through it all, he continued to ride her, making sure she didn't come down from the high he'd inspired.

"That was amazing, Sterling," he crooned. "I bet you can do it again for me. Can't you, baby girl?"

Whispered encouragements had her straining against him, yearning for more, intent on being the woman of his dreams if only for this one encounter.

Instead of slaking her thirst for him, that first release only took the edge off her wild desire, making her more aware of the rapture he granted her as he continued to build her higher once more with careful, measured strokes.

After a few minutes, she whimpered, wishing their position—not to mention their mostly dressed state—didn't limit his thrusts. As if he could read her frustration, he responded, walking with her, still joined, to the cab of the truck. He kicked off his jeans and boots in the process, miraculously managing not to dump both their asses in the dust, leaving himself completely nude.

When he yanked open the door, she realized what he intended. With one last eyeful of his glorious frame, she turned as he lifted her and nudged her shoulder. The motion dislodged his cock, and they both groaned.

Sterling shouldn't have worried about the emptiness since he quickly situated her so she knelt on the edge of the truck's floor and bent over the seat. Her skirt bunched around her waist with her ass in the air. After running his hand over her backside and humming his approval, Viho climbed onto the running board of the truck and reintroduced his hard-on, which felt even plumper after its brief absence.

Sterling tangled her hands in the passenger seatbelts, loving the way they wrapped around her wrists to keep her secure in the wake of Viho's escalating fucking. From this angle he drove deeper, harder than he had before. She loved every second. Especially when he fisted her hair and drew her head back, arching her neck.

With the other, he grabbed the oh-shit handle and used the leverage to increase the pace and travel of his lunges. His hips slapped her ass as he picked up speed. Her breasts rubbed against the faux leather seat as he jackhammered into her from behind.

Then his hand released her hair and wandered down her back and over her hip. He wormed his fingers between her belly and the seat so they could toy with her clit. Drawing circles around the tiny nub, he pushed her over the edge. Again.

Sterling screamed his name as she shattered around him, humping his hand so that she ground her clit on his skilled fingers and wrung every bit of ecstasy his fat shaft delivered. He shuttled in and out of her as if unaffected by her desire.

Never had she been with a man who had as much control as Viho.

Maybe because he was significantly older than the guys she'd been with.

Maybe just because he was special.

Either way, she planned to give as good as she got.

As soon as she could breathe again. She shuddered as she collapsed onto the seat with a keening moan that ended on a whimper.

"Don't worry, I'm not finished with you yet," he growled in her ear as he lifted her from the truck and cradled her in his arms. He nuzzled her forehead with his chin, then marched to the tailgate of the truck, leaping inside the bed it as if it were merely a curb to hop.

He set her on her feet briefly as he fluffed out the rolled blanket she'd spied earlier. The traditional patterns, along with the distinct red, black and white coloring of the cloth, made her sure he'd brought it with him from the reservation. It had character and an unevenness that spoke of being hand-woven natural fibers versus something synthetic or factory bought. As a craftsman herself, she could appreciate the effort it must have taken to make.

In less than a minute, he unfurled the sleeping bag and laid it out, making as comfy a spot to lie as she required. Hell, she'd gladly have gotten on all fours in the dirt by the road if it would have made him hurry.

More than anything, she wanted to keep feeling. The overwhelming rush of sensations made it easy to forget everything logical. Painful.

Sterling didn't wait. She squirmed from Viho's hold despite his attempts to cling to her wriggling body. Good, she liked that he wanted her as much as she wanted him. "Just long enough to get totally naked, I promise."

She smiled as she shimmied out of her skirt, then unbuttoned her black lace shirt. The tank top below disappeared over her head in no time, leaving her modeling a matching pink satin bra and panty set.

Clearly a naked kind of guy, Viho didn't display any hint of embarrassment when he approached her, fully, gloriously nude. She didn't blame him. Sterling could have looked at him all day and never gotten bored. In fact, she took a mental snapshot, hoping to sketch it later.

Stalking closer, Viho scanned her from head to toe. He paused only long enough to draw his knuckles along the gray feathers dangling from her earrings to the tops of her breasts before reaching behind her to unfasten her bra.

Once he'd slipped her free of the contraption and dropped it to the ground, he looked at her long and hard. Her nipples pebbled as he admired her bare breasts and her naked spirit.

"So damn young. Pretty," he rasped quietly, as if to himself, before claiming her lips once again. And she got distracted before she could get rid of her panties.

The yarn of his blanket was soft against her back as he guided her onto it and followed her down. Then all thoughts fled, except the pressure of him on top of her. Perfect and delicious. Fooling around like they had, fast and rough, was great, but this—making love to him face to face, without the sexual gymnastics—allowed them both to relax into the moment.

He guided his cock to her wet slit and traced the furrow of her pussy, reacclimating her sensitive flesh to his presence.

This time they didn't crack jokes, second-guess themselves or pause to think better. They let their bodies do the talking, making out as they got comfortable. Weight, heat and the pressure of Viho's thigh nestling between Sterling's legs before spreading them around the trunk of his body each should have freaked her out. None of it did. It only turned her on more.

Bold, she snaked her hand between them, weighing his heavy balls in her palm. She rolled his sac lightly, swallowing his approving groan before moving on to cup his erection. Squeezing it and measuring the impressive length with a couple gliding strokes from root to tip. Her thumb swiped a bead of precome from the slit in the head before bringing it to her lips for a taste.

It was as if sex with him was the first genuine encounter she'd ever had. Uninhibited, she let all of herself loose. And he didn't seem to mind one bit.

His finger slipped beneath the elastic of her panties. She arched upward, into his touch.

Then the last scrap of fabric separating them disappeared as he ripped them from her and tossed them somewhere.

Viho kissed her neck as she dragged air into her lungs. He tapped her clit with the damp head of his cock, teasing her before fitting himself to her once more.

"Come with me this time?" she asked, suddenly wanting nothing more than to share the beautiful explosion with him.

"Yeah. Gotta." He clenched his jaw as he buried himself fully within her sheath. "You're too damn perfect not to. Making me crazy."

"Good." She smiled as she stroked his cheek then buried her fingers in his lush mane. "I'm not alone, then."

"No. Definitely not." He stared into her eyes as he worked them both toward the frenzy of release. "I'm right here with you."

As if that promise was more alluring than anything he'd done to her body, Sterling quaked. Her pussy clenched, her muscles undulating as she tried to suck him deeper. She wrapped her legs around him, her heels drumming his tight ass in time to the perfect rhythm he set for them.

And right then she knew, she'd never have sex this good with anyone else in her lifetime.

They were a perfect match in bed. Or in a truck bed. However that went.

Completely in tune, Viho ramped up the rocking of their bodies, escalating the connection between them. Perspiration made their skin glide, reducing friction and enhancing their motion.

Perfect balance, totally in sync. Effortless, reciprocal pleasure.

They generated it together.

So Sterling felt it the instant Viho's stride hitched. She clamped her legs around him when he seemed like he would retreat. "Where do you think you're going?"

"I'm going to come." A bead of sweat trickled down his face.

"Good. Me too." She yanked him to her, whispering against his lips, "Don't leave. Come. Inside me. I want to feel you let go. Give it to me."

Viho shouted, then went mad. He grasped her shoulders to anchor her, then pounded inside her, reaching as deep as possible with his steely cock. Sterling cried her triumph into the country air.

When he went stiff above her, she knew he'd surrendered. And she'd already begun to quake as the first blast of his semen painted a line across the inside of her pussy. He matched her spasm for spasm as he filled her with jets of come.

She came so hard around him that she'd swear it was the night sky full of stars hanging above her. Or maybe she was about to pass out. Either way, she'd never had a dream as good as this one.

When he'd finished flooding her, Viho collapsed.

He smothered her with a flurry of kisses and words in a language she didn't understand. She didn't need to know what they meant to catch his intent, though.

They cuddled together, recovering for a while. Viho rolled them up in the red, white and black blanket like a post-coital burrito. Instead of feeling trapped, Sterling felt protected. Shielded from the negativity she'd wallowed in before Viho illuminated her world with light and life.

Plus, oh-my-God level orgasms.

As they lay in the quiet air, she snuggled into his side, pleased to see his ribs still expanding rapidly from his exertion. Smug, she melted into him. And that was when she realized her phone was ringing. First, the ridiculous *bleep* she'd assigned to one of her cousins intruded. She ignored it. Completely incapable of moving. And without the will to leave Viho's side.

A little bit passed. Then another one of her cousins called.

Still she pretended not to hear.

And then something way more urgent shattered her peaceful calm.

Her dad's bold, insistent ringtone.

Oh shit.

Sterling bolted upright. Well, she tried anyway. Mostly she choked herself on the edge of the blanket. Gurgling and flopping around like a fish, she finally got Viho's attention.

"What's wrong?" He flipped open the blanket and rolled onto his knees, immediately poised for battle. But there was nothing around them, infringing on their solitude.

"That's my dad. Shit. Shit. Fuck." She hopped across the stones toward her Jeep, cursing as each rock drilled into her tender arches.

Viho lay back and laughed, folding his arms

across his ripped belly. "You're a damn fine grown woman. You don't have to be running at your daddy's beck and call. Not that I'm complaining about the show you and your jiggly parts are putting on right about now. Settle down. It's not like he actually caught us with our pants down. You haven't done anything wrong, have you? You aren't married, are you?"

"Shit, no. Nothing like that. But you don't understand. I told my family I'd spotted you out here. I never imagined we'd…take our time like that." Sterling fumbled the door and lunged for her phone. Too late. It'd stopped ringing. *Damn!* "Believe me, nothing is worse than one of the infamous Compass Brothers when he's worried about his damn daughter."

Viho quit laughing as quickly as he'd started. His voice lost all traces of warmth and ease when he barked, "*Compass?*"

"Yeah, I'm Sterling Compton. My dad is Sam, one of the Compass Brothers from Compass Ranch. Have you heard of him? I swear most of the stories are embellished. He hasn't actually murdered any of my boyfriends. But between him and my uncles, I guaran-fucking-tee you the cavalry is on the way. I suggest you put your jeans on as quick as you took them off unless you want to meet my father buck-ass naked."

Chapter Four

And wasn't that just fucking perfect?

Viho banged his head on the bed of the truck. Not only had he managed to break down near the one town in the whole damn state he'd tried like hell to avoid, but he'd also fucking *fucked* the daughter of one of the very few men on Earth that he hated. And not in some messed-up revenge scheme sort of way, either. He wasn't that kind of asshole.

He stared at his still half-hard dick—which really appreciated the view of Sterling's pert ass peeking from behind the door of her Jeep despite the bomb she'd inadvertently dropped—and cursed it for liking the young woman so much.

Young.

Woman.

She had to be fifteen years his junior. Had he let that stop him when she'd offered herself up like the most delicious and unexpected treat he'd ever devoured?

Sure hadn't.

Now he would pay. This is what happened when you ignored common sense.

Yet some part of him figured it'd probably been worth all the trouble sleeping with her was about to cause him. Because it had been amazing. She had been. The sex too, but mostly her. Adventurous, sweet, generous, wild…everything he'd ever wanted in a woman.

And she had to be a damn Compass Girl.

Fuck my life.

At least his mother wasn't around to see him screw up so majorly after being cautious the rest of his life. He fingered the blanket she'd woven, one of her favorites. Heart heavy, he didn't hear Sterling scrambling back toward him until she'd leapt into the truck bed.

She snatched her skirt and delicate top from the floor and dusted them off as best she could before slipping into them. He mourned the loss of the view while she covered up her pale, petal-soft skin.

"Aren't you going to get dressed?" She gaped at him. Every hint of the doe-eyed innocence she'd aimed at him minutes ago vanished. "Seriously, Jade texted me Code Red twenty-five minutes ago. My dad probably stopped by the main house for something, ran into my cousins and figured out what was up. He could be here any second."

"I'm not ashamed of what we did. But I don't want to cause you any trouble either." Viho hated the disappointment creeping in. He tried not to allow people to let him down anymore. He reached into a giant duffle bag behind him and withdrew a clean shirt, tugging it over his head.

He hopped over the side of the truck, then snagged his jeans and boots. He tugged them on, fastened the button with one hand, then vaulted back beside Sterling.

She attempted to straighten her hair, which didn't do much to erase the effects of their romp or the wind that had whipped through her open window earlier. He dug into the bag again and withdrew a bone comb.

"Let me." He sat with his legs crossed, tugging Sterling into the diamond between his crotch and his ankles. She fit perfectly in his hold.

Taking his time, he swiped the stray hair from her forehead, aligning it down her back. It would have to suffice as a thank you, and a goodbye. At least from a personal perspective. Because in a few minutes, he'd have to put a hell of a lot of distance between them.

It wasn't safe for them to associate with each other.

The least he could do was tend to her, soothing the disturbance he'd caused in her world in the past hour. Starting from the bottom, in the small of her back, he gently worked the tangles from her silky strands. Having long hair himself, he knew what it felt like to catch a snarl on a hastily wielded brush and he didn't dare subject her to even that minor discomfort.

It was bad enough that their afterglow had been obliterated.

Sterling relaxed into his care as he hummed softly and tended to her. He admitted to himself that he made several unnecessary passes through her hair simply because he didn't want to let her go any sooner than he had to.

"Viho?" she asked softly.

"Yeah."

"Why do you have all your things back here?" Her hand wandered blindly backward until she squeezed his knee. "Are you living out of your truck?"

"I guess you could say I'm in transition." Evasive maneuvers were in order.

"Does that mean homeless?" she wondered. When she tried to turn and face him, he held her shoulders in place, pretending to comb imaginary knots.

"Temporarily. I haven't found where I'm

supposed to be yet." That was the truth. Drifting. He'd lost his anchor, like he'd told her before. Except he didn't ever expect he'd find another home when the one person he'd cared about was gone. His mother. Dead.

"Do you hear a motor?" Sterling perked up. She stood, glancing out onto the horizon. "Yep. Incoming. There they are."

"They?"

"That's Jake's truck. He's my dad's best friend. Anyway, his rig is better for towing. My dad is the ranch's business manager. Should have figured they'd come together. As if I need both of them giving me grief."

"Jake?" Viho would have banged his skull some more if Sterling hadn't turned to look at him with her cute head tipped just a bit to the left. "Jake Cartwright?"

"Yes. He's worked on our ranch forever. More than twenty-five years. Even before my mom moved there while my dad was working in New York City. You seem to know a lot about our set up. Were you hoping for work? I'd be glad to put in a good word—"

"No!" He waved her off. "No way. That's not what this was about."

"Of course not, you didn't know who I was… Well, I guess Sterling isn't exactly a common name." She frowned. "You didn't know. Did you?"

"Hell no." Viho accidentally knocked into her shoulder as he bolted past and jumped down from the truck. "I don't need to fuck the boss's daughter to land a job. I wouldn't take it even if they offered. Not in a million years. I just need a ride into town. I'll figure something out from there."

"Hey, don't freak out. It's like you said, they don't know what we were doing out here. And it's not like my dad would shoot you for sleeping with me or something." Sterling crossed her fingers mostly behind her back, probably thinking he couldn't see.

"We're about to find out." In approximately twenty seconds, the shit was going to hit the fan.

If Jake recognized Viho…

Odds were he wouldn't.

Viho prayed the guy wouldn't.

Over and over. And over.

Because a confrontation of that magnitude was definitely not on his agenda for today.

Then again, neither breaking down in the middle of nowhere nor finding an angel and fucking her on the side of the road had been either. Only the awesomeness of that last one helped ease the sting of the rest.

Behind him, Sterling had realized she still was barefoot. She sprinted gingerly to her boots and stomped into them, hopefully behind the cover of his oafish body. Dual slams echoed through the wilderness, setting birds into flight from nearby scrubby bushes.

"Sterling!" Sam Compton bellowed. More in question than greeting. The man glared at Viho as he approached, his face contorted into something mean until he caught sight of his daughter, who trotted over to meet him, perfectly unharmed.

"Hi, Dad!" She hugged the tall guy—fit for his age and supposed bookishness—around his middle. "Thanks for coming."

"What the hell have you been doing out here that you couldn't stop and answer your damn phone?" Sam returned his daughter's hug with interest, nuzzling the crown of her head even as he berated her. He paused, sniffing her hair as if he could detect Viho's scent on her.

Don't be paranoid, Chief.

"I was trying to fix his engine, but it's no good." Sterling attempted to shrug where her father smothered her. "Be nice, Daddy."

The man looked up and his eyes held no sliver of the warmth he'd reserved for his daughter. Menacing, he practically snarled.

Viho took a deep breath and manned up. He approached the pair with his hand extended. "Nice to meet you, sir."

"Sam Compton." He enveloped Viho with a grip that didn't kid around. Viho returned the shake with interest.

"Viho." He didn't dare give his surname. Not with Jake closing in from the other side of the truck. Viho didn't dare so much as glance at the man. Though he had a desperate urge to steal a peek. It was too dangerous.

If they recognized him, they'd surely leave him there to rot. And despite his wishes otherwise, he admitted that he needed their help. Damn them.

Having met two of the cursed Comptons now, he could understand the draw. Part of him would never truly forgive Jake, but he could see where the whole family, their operation and this place, did have some allure.

How could he think that? After a lifetime of bitterness, one interlude with a Compass siren couldn't possibly alter his perspective, could it?

His mother had always discouraged his rage. But he couldn't help it.

Despite her protests that Jake had never known. That she'd run off before telling him the truth. Viho just couldn't understand. Because if he found someone to love, he'd never let them go so easily.

And standing there now, all he could think was that his mother would have done anything to have witnessed this moment. While he would do anything to avoid it.

"Viho?" Sterling nudged him, making him aware that he'd spaced out for a moment. "You okay?"

"Sorry, it's been a long day out here. Not as hot as it has been, but dry." He offered up a lame facsimile of a smile and shrugged.

He would have turned away but Sterling had to display her manners. "This is my honorary uncle, Jake."

And Viho couldn't avoid it for another moment.

The guy proffered his hand.

Viho swallowed hard. He took a huge breath, then shook, allowing his gaze to wander up to the man's face. He prepared for a million different emotions.

Rage. Rejection. Disbelief. Sorrow.

Instead, there was nothing.

No hint of recognition.

Polite indifference cut deeper than anything else could have.

"Nice to meet you, son." The guy shook hard.

"Don't call me that," was all Viho could manage before yanking his arm back as if scorched. He spun on his heel and acted busy so he didn't lose his mind. Hell, he was probably closer to Jake's age than Sterling's. Or at least it seemed that way. This whole situation was fucked up beyond belief.

Out of the corner of his eye, he saw Sam shrug at his best friend. Sterling jogged to catch Viho as he rounded the hood and slammed it closed.

"Play it cool. You're acting weird for nothing." She touched his elbow lightly. Again he shook her off.

"It ain't nothing. Maybe you all should leave me here and head back home," he grumbled.

"Don't be ridiculous," Sterling said at the same time her father approached and asked, "You worried about money?"

Viho grunted, "Can't say I have anything to repay

you with."

It was true.

Plus, it might get rid of them sooner. There had to be a better Plan B.

Except it seemed the ruder he was, the more they tried to kill him with kindness.

"You look like a strong worker to me," Jake piped up. "I'm always looking for guys willing to earn an honest paycheck. What do you do?"

"Uh." Somehow that caught him off guard.

"If you don't have skills we can train you, no problem." Sam smiled kindly, not unlike his daughter. "It doesn't take a lot of experience to muck stalls."

"I'm plenty capable of using a shovel. Actually, I do landscaping." He wasn't sure why he admitted that as he knocked his fist on the faded outline of the lettering he'd peeled off his truck last week when he'd left the reservation for good.

"Did you hear that shit, Sam?" Jake laughed as he thumped himself on the chest.

Was his ruse up? Did Jake actually know the truth?

Viho froze.

But Sterling twirled on her toes, grinning. "This is perfect! My grandmother has been harping on my dad to hire a gardener. Someone to restore her flowers around the main house. She…"

Sterling went pale.

"She's ill," Sam finished for her, reaching out to put a hand on his daughter's shoulder. "Alzheimer's. She keeps forgetting that we let the vegetable patch and flower garden go years ago."

He swallowed hard and looked to Jake.

"Mrs. Compton would love to see her handiwork restored. What do you say? We'll haul your truck in, give you a place to stay and a steady paycheck." Jake offered. "It's so late in the season now, you'll have to order and place mature plants. Get everything winterized in a few months. Maybe stay on until spring to tend to the blooms. By then you'll have yourself a new truck and can continue on your way."

Sterling grinned as she hugged Jake.

The sight stole Viho's ability to think rationally. Surreal.

The whole day overwhelmed him.

And he started to believe that childish dreams could come true. It was like he'd fallen down a rabbit hole. Part of him didn't want to leave again, returning to a cold and empty world.

So he watched from outside his body as some foolish part of him surrendered to wishful thinking and he muttered aloud, "I don't have many other options, do I?"

"Say yes," Sterling urged him. The wicked light in her eyes alone should have scared him away. This was too dangerous of a game. And she didn't even know they were playing it.

But Viho supposed it didn't matter. He could take the job if Jake really didn't know who he was. Working on the ranch would be like stabbing himself repeatedly with a rusty knife. Some sick part of him was curious, though. What was the guy really like?

Viho would find out. He'd do what he had to and then move on like he'd originally planned.

With no one the wiser.

Especially not Jake.

"Okay." He nodded. Against all his better judgment he croaked, "Yes. I accept. Thank you."

Sam Compton smiled. He squinted a bit as he looked from Viho to Jake then back again, but Sterling's squeal distracted him. She clapped, then beamed up at her father. "This is going to be great. I can't wait to tell Vivi."

And then her face fell.

Her bottom lip trembled.

All three men reached for her.

"Shit. Dad." Her voice broke. Viho wanted to hug her, but Sam beat him to it. "There's something I have to tell you. I—I almost forgot."

She pressed a hand to her forehead as if she couldn't believe it. And Viho knew that whatever had driven her into his arms was about to be out in the open.

As intimate as they'd been with each other, he knew the other two men would think it weird if he butted in on family business, so he busied himself with preparing the truck for towing.

Sam and Sterling stepped aside, lowering their voices as they shared whatever bad news it was she had to break to her father. From the way the guy sat, hard, in the dirt, Viho figured it was pretty terrible.

Jake clearly wanted to join them, if the thousand times he glanced over his shoulder was any indication. Instead, he busted his ass, setting up the tow, presumably so they could get the hell home and figure out their business. In private.

Quietly, the two guys worked together, Viho's mind reeling from the sheer oddity of the feeling. He stepped in time to Jake, both of them doing things in the same way, as if they'd learned them together. In no time, they were ready to go.

It was impossible to miss the trail of tears making silver streaks down Sterling's face when he glanced over at her.

"Ride with me?" she asked Viho as she passed by.

"Of course." He didn't hesitate for a moment.

"Thanks. I'll be in the Jeep." She sniffled, then strode away.

Sam Compton joined Viho and Jake, looking rough himself. Gone was the jovial guy and the protective father. Instead, he kind of looked like he could use a hug himself.

Viho could relate.

The guy made it hard to hate him.

Hard, but not impossible.

They'd finished hooking the truck up and were rounding the back end when Sam glanced up in one final double-check. The way he stutter-stepped gave him away. He'd seen something he didn't like. Viho couldn't afford a disaster. The truck might be junk, but it—and the meager belongings it held—was all he had. Salvage value might get him a couple hundred bucks closer to the exit in this screwed up situation.

He glanced at the connections, finding them solid, then tracked the Compass Brother's line of sight. Straight to the torn wreckage of Sterling's panties, which waved like a flag from the bed of the truck. When they'd jacked it up, the shifting gear had revealed the lacy carnage as clearly as a neon sign.

Viho whipped his head around to find Sam staring at him now, with crossed arms that made him look more like an asskicker than a nerd. Viho offered up an awkward shrug before glancing away from the accusation in Sam Compton's eyes and found something even more threatening in the knowing stare of Jake Cartwright.

While Viho could brush off the raised hackles of a protective dad, it was a hell of a lot harder to dismiss a condemning glare from the one man who should have had *his* back unconditionally.

Then again, he'd always known his father—Jake *fucking* Cartwright—had hated the very idea of him because the loser had never bothered to meet his own son. Or cared enough about the lovesick woman he'd ruined for life to find out why she'd disappeared in the middle of a random night and raced back to a family who'd disapproved of her "sordid" affair with someone outside their inner circle.

Viho spun on his heel before he did something rash. Like deck the guy.

No respect.

Viho had none for Jake, whose laser stare singed Viho's retreating back as he climbed into the Jeep with Sterling. That didn't make it hurt any less.

Fuck this town. Fuck these people.

Except the woman who looked at him with kind and remorseful eyes despite her own private catastrophe, whatever that might be. She patted his thigh before starting her car and pointing them toward town, leaving her father and honorary uncle behind, though she couldn't possibly have known how badly he needed the reassurance of her gentle touch.

He hoped he could do what he had to and escape this nightmare—his own personal hell—without hurting her.

From where he was sitting, it seemed like an impossible task.

Viho dropped his head back against the rest and closed his eyes as he frantically tried to concoct a plan for surviving the next several months. Hell, the next several hours.

It sure as shit wasn't going to be easy.

Chapter Five

Viho peeked between the branches of the rosebush he was pruning when he caught sight of killer legs wrapped in skinny jeans. He hoped for a glimpse of the woman they belonged to, remembering how they'd felt hugging his hips. Sterling. He subtly adjusted his insta-hard-on before mindlessly snipping a wayward sprig riddled with thorns.

She was torturing him.

Every day, she toured the garden with her grandmother, praising his work and enjoying the product of his labor. He admitted to himself that the grounds were coming along, but her kind words only made him feel like more of a prick for ignoring her. Or appearing to.

It'd been six weeks since she'd found him on the side of the road like garbage someone had tossed out. Except she hadn't treated him like he was worthless.

The first few days he'd worked on the ranch, she'd gone out of her way to welcome him and make it clear that she would've gone right on making him happier than he'd remembered being in a long time. Maybe ever.

Viho couldn't accept her gracious offer of comfort or companionship. Not when he hid so many secrets—and a truckload of resentment for her father, uncles and especially Jake—from her.

It wouldn't be fair.

Besides, the gap in their ages was almost ridiculous—it was so big. A fourteen-year difference. He'd never escape Compass Ranch without getting his ass kicked if their affair leaked. The list of reasons why he couldn't have her stretched longer than the inventory of plants Mrs. Compton had approved for her expansive gardens. So he'd distanced himself, then focused on his duties.

Hell, the job was big enough to last a reasonable landscaper a lifetime. And he could have been content maintaining his design after installing it too. If it didn't require tending to enemy territory. Just one more thing to resent, really.

Viho closed his eyes in an attempt to block out the negativity threatening to blacken his soul. He had to survive this fall, maybe a few more seasons, and then he could be on his way. He realized now why Sam, Jake and Sterling had been in such a hurry, insisting on the late season planting of the flowers.

Mrs. Compton wasn't going to be around much longer.

Every day she was delighted anew by the progress that had been made. A glorious surprise for her to wake to each morning, having forgotten its existence from the day before. Viho couldn't help himself. As much as he despised Jake and the non-blood family that had kept the guy away from his own, he admired Sterling Compton.

The love and support she lavished on her grandmother couldn't be construed as anything but respectable. Having cared for his own mother as she faded away, suffering from cancer, he understood how painful the long-term care of a relative could be. Every day, he had to stuff his hands in his pockets as Sterling strolled by to keep from bundling her in his arms and squeezing her tight, murmuring his encouragement.

In his mind, he held her, rocking her as they sat here, between the rows of blossoms.

Lost in his fantasy, he didn't hear the two women approach until it was too late to duck into another section of the garden.

"Viho." Sterling's greeting lacked the warmth of her initial overtures. She'd slowly chilled to downright frosty toward him when she realized he didn't intend to return her affection. He couldn't blame her. It was for the best.

Even if he despised it.

"Hey, Sterling. Mrs. Compton." He nodded at the women and hoped they'd pass quickly to the table under the tall oak tree where they usually sipped a glass of iced tea together as they talked.

"Jake?" Vicky squinted as if even she knew the error of her declaration.

Viho quickly corrected her, so off balance by her simple mistake that he plopped onto his ass in the dirt. "No, ma'am."

A wince creased Sterling's pretty face as she debated whether to explain. Most times lately the family seemed to have given up, letting their precious Vivi believe as she would. It had to get exhausting to repeat the truth, knowing she'd forget it a moment later. Though she still could recall things that had happened in the past year or two, her short-term memory had all but disintegrated.

Her disease reminded Viho of a memory-eating monster, who started its meal with the freshest information. Its appetite grew as it went, erasing more and more from Mrs. Compton's mind. About a month ago he'd even seen her grow angry, shattering a glass by throwing it against the tree when frustration overcame her. Now she seemed resigned. Or maybe she'd simply forgotten how she used to be.

Sterling settled for simple. "This is our landscaper, Viho."

"Funny, he has eyes like Jake." The perceptive old woman called him out, making him duck his head so she couldn't detect any other similarities.

"I know, Vivi. I've thought so too." Sterling's friendly tone had him peeking up again in time to see her soft smile. "They're nice, right?"

"Almost as beautiful as all these flowers, though I'm sure a man hates to be called gorgeous. So I'll say this, Mr. Viho—you're doing a fine job." Mrs. Compton leaned over to pat him on the back with her gnarled fingers. Somehow the gesture infused him with warmth. And pride in his work. "Thank you."

Throat tight, Viho had to stare at the ground once more. This time for entirely different reasons. Sweat rolled down his forehead, more from the intensity of his emotions than the surprising burst of heat on the sunny fall day.

"A man gets awful thirsty when performing hard labor. You should join us for a drink." Mrs. Compton, ever a lady, invited him to their gathering.

"I couldn't. I've got a lot more work to do before I lose the light." He panicked, twisting around and clipping a dead branch. At least, that's what he intended, but with his shaking hands, he slipped and stabbed himself instead. Not anything major considering the scrapes, bumps, bruises and punctures he endured every day. A hazard of working outdoors.

But the women squeaked when blood began to well from the wound.

"Viho! You're bleeding." Sterling gasped.

"You'd better come clean that cut out," Vicky

suggested. "You don't want to get an infection."

"Seriously, your hands are slathered in dirt and those shears are a little rusty," Sterling piled on.

Viho tucked the offending instrument under the pile of cuttings so they couldn't see the terrible shape of his tools. It'd been in his plan to buy new ones. Eventually.

Still, they balked when he yanked his shirt over his head and wrapped it around the injury. Damn, it did sting. He could have kicked himself for being careless and making the situation worse. Sterling blinked a few times, then her gaze wandered along his muscles to the bulge in his pants.

Terrific.

"Come on." She took his elbow and led him to the table as if he were as feeble as Vicky.

"It's not a big deal." He stopped just short of rolling his eyes at her when she pressed his shoulders, coaxing him to sit so she could fuss over him.

He'd be lying if he didn't say that some shred of him enjoyed her attention. Another part of him entirely wished he could swipe everything off the table with one arm and have her again, right here, right now.

Well, except for her grandmother looking on.

"Let me see." Sterling knelt between his legs, not helping abate his fantasies.

She lifted his hand from his thigh, took it in hers and dribbled ice water over the injury, washing away the stain on his skin. He wished she could remove the blemishes on his heart as easily.

Despite the fact that he was fine, he let her tend to the wound, cleaning and wrapping it in a strip of cotton from his ruined shirt.

"All good now," she announced when she'd finished the field dressing.

"Thank you." He couldn't stop himself from

cupping her cheek in his other hand. Unfortunately, that only got her dirty. Damn.

He yanked his fingers back, though she giggled and swiped the mess from her cheek with the remains of his tee. Was it his imagination, or did she pause to smell the fabric for an instant?

Out of nowhere, Vicky raised her voice, "Do you have a girlfriend, Mr....?"

"Viho," he reminded her.

"Right." The older woman grinned. "You two look kind of nice together. I wouldn't object if you wanted to take my granddaughter on a date, you know."

"Vivi!" Sterling shot her a look that was equal parts mortification and outrage.

The lady simply laughed. And though it was awkward, Viho was happy he'd had a part in making her smile.

"What's all this fun? Why wasn't I invited?" Hope ambled over with Wyatt and Clayton, two of the ranch hands Viho had gotten to know over the past several weeks. The guys seemed competent, honorable and totally in love with Sterling's cousin. They were engaged to her. Both of them.

Viho was impressed with how open-minded the family was to the unconventional relationship until he'd learned that one of the Compass Brothers—Silas, the head of the ranch—had a wife *and* a husband.

Some of the things he'd told himself about how horrible these people must be to lure his father away from him all these years had clearly been lies. Immature feelings borne of hurt. They hammered home to him just how narrow-minded his community had been. And how different most people were from that.
Understanding that reality had cost Viho. But it didn't diminish his jealousy.

All his life, he'd wished for what these people

had.

"Just the usual picnic in the garden. Except Viho hurt himself." Sterling bit her lip, frowning.

"I'm fine. Better get back to work, actually." He started to rise.

Wyatt stopped him with a heavy hand on his shoulder. "Take a break, man. Maybe hang around until Sienna shows up. She's a nurse. You should have that checked out. I made a similar mistake recently, underestimating a flesh wound. Trust me, you don't want to go through what I did."

"He's not joking. His hand was like a watermelon. He could have lost it. Or worse," Clay added. "Take care of yourself. You're working like the Compass Brothers are slave drivers."

Wasn't Viho essentially an indentured servant? He shook his head at the terrible thought. The Comptons had treated him fairly. More than.

"Besides, our little brothers are headed this way in a second and they'll die if you disappear. Bryant and Austin have been rattling on non-stop about all the plant stuff you've been teaching them for survival training. I've heard about it every night at dinner this week." Hope smiled at Viho.

He'd have to be more careful what he shared with the boys. They were so eager to study, he'd let his guard down, sharing facts he'd learned from other members of his tribe who'd taken him under their wing when he'd had no one of his own to instruct him in their ways.

Sure enough, two kids spirited across the main house's manicured lawn, unintentionally tearing up some of the patches he'd put down to fill in bare spots.

"Hey, guys! Don't mess up Viho's seeds." Sterling looked to him and mouthed, *Sorry.*

He shrugged, wondering what it would have been

like to grow up carefree. "It's not a problem."

Right behind them, Sam Compton approached more calmly, holding hands with his wife, Cindi. They too scolded the boys to be more careful. The only way this impromptu gathering could get any worse would be if Jake strolled up. Thankfully, he didn't.

Sam kissed his mother on the cheek, then turned toward the rest of them. "Hey, Viho. Could I ask you a favor?"

"Of course, boss." He prayed for anything to get him out of this situation, where he wanted to fit in too fucking much for comfort.

"I know it's not in your job description, but I promised Sterling I'd help her with some fixtures she's moving into the expanded area of her shop." He looked at his daughter then. "Sorry, but I have a meeting that just came up. I can't do it today. And I know I've already put it off a few times."

"It's okay, Dad. I can do it myself. More hands would have made the job quicker, that's all." She shrugged.

"Don't you dare lug those display cases around by yourself." He pointed his finger at her and wagged it. "Last time you were limping for a week after pulling a stunt like that. Besides, your mom told me you haven't been feeling so great this week."

Viho couldn't stand the thought of Sterling hurting herself.

"It's no problem. I can help," he blurted out.

"Thanks." Sam slapped him on the back as he headed toward the offices in the barn. "Tell Jake to mark you down for overtime."

"That's not necessary." He waved off the generosity. Sterling's glare made it clear what she thought of his assistance, paid or otherwise.

"Seriously, Dad, it's not. I'm fine on my own!"

She crossed her arms, yelling to be heard as Sam grew farther away.

"Don't be stubborn, Sterling. You get that from your mom, you know?" he shouted to her as he retreated. "Love you. Don't take it out on Viho just 'cause you're pissed at me."

"What's his problem?" Jade asked as she hauled over a chair and plopped into it, her guy, Liam, standing behind her. Sienna showed up too, with her husband, Daniel. Viho hadn't even seen her car roll into the lot.

He had to get the hell out of there before any more of the Comptons swarmed around them. He looked at Sterling. "Come on, let's do this."

"Are you sure one of you can't help me reconfigure the shop instead of making me bug Viho?" Sterling practically begged her cousins and the guys who loved them.

"Nope. Gotta wash my hair or something," Jade obviously lied.

"And we're going to be busy…" Hope hooked her arm through the elbow of each of her mates. Everyone on the ranch was talking about how she wanted to get pregnant. They apparently were *busy* a lot.

"Viho's definitely the guy for this job." Sienna stared pointedly at her cousin. "So get the hell out of here you two, would you please?"

Why did he get the feeling that they were being set up? Not by Sam. But by Sterling's cousins, definitely. Had she told them about their clandestine afternoon? And could they seriously be okay with that despite their age difference or how he'd treated her since?

Viho appreciated their vote of confidence, but he didn't deserve it.

Damn, they *all* made it impossible to abhor them. No matter how hard he tried. He wanted to laugh and punch something at the same time. So he got up and started walking toward Sterling's Jeep as if he were walking the plank on a ship.

Because he was pretty sure where being alone with Sterling would land them, if she didn't knee him in the balls first.

A few moments later, she caught up, trotting to match his long strides.

Steeped in awkward silence, they wandered toward her Jeep.

Together, yet not.

Chapter Six

The instant they were alone in the truck, Sterling whipped around to face him. "I'm taking you straight home."

"Like hell. I promised your dad—"

"Whatever. I don't need your pity." She damn near pouted. It was more sexy than annoying, though. "I'm not going to force you to spend time with me when you're clearly not interested. Let's save us both the embarrassment and discomfort."

"Ah, shit. Sterling, I'm sorry stuff between us went the way it did. I would never have slept with you if I'd known how things were going to turn out. You know, that you were a Compass Girl or that I'd be working here. You can't imagine how far out of the realm of possibility I thought that was." He scrubbed his hand over his face.

"Why was I good enough before, but not after, you knew who I was?" she calmed down enough to ask him directly.

Viho preferred her riled. This was harder to combat.

There was nothing he could tell her that would alleviate the recrimination in her tone or the doubt in her eyes without sharing the truth. That was not a possibility.

When he didn't respond, she angled the Jeep toward the bunkhouse he'd been sharing with a couple of other single guys.

"Wait. Seriously, I want to help you out, Sterling. Not because I told your dad I would, either."

She slowed.

"Can you please accept this as the peace offering it is? I don't regret having sex with you. Son of a bitch, it was the best day I've had in a long time and I'll remember it for the rest of my life." He reached over and touched the metal cuff on her wrist. It was beautiful, like her.

He knew by looking at it that she'd made it.

And despite his better judgment, he wanted to know more about her profession. To see *her* work, and where she created these things, interested him. So the excuse to do it under the guise of assisting her... Well, it was all fine by him.

Sterling drew a deep breath, then three-pointed it in the middle of the ranch road. Though her mouth formed a stern slash that didn't look at all like her usual glowing smile, she accepted his offer. "Fine. But it isn't going to be any fun. This shit is heavy. And I'm not going to feel bad when you're hurting tomorrow."

He *really* wanted to crack a joke about them getting sore together, but he kept it to himself. Good thing too, if the derisive glance she threw him was any clue to how she felt. It threatened to shrivel his balls where he sat.

Viho kept his mouth shut the entire ride into town. It was nice to get away for a few hours. He truly didn't want to admit it, not even to himself, but the ranch had an awesome set up. The hands he'd met were pretty cool men too. In no time at all, they'd picked up his old nickname from the few elders on the reservation who'd taught him all he knew. The ones who'd respected him and his hunger for learning the true old ways. *Chief.*

But six weeks without wheels—or even a horse—had just about driven him nuts.

The only saving grace, when he wasn't working overtime on Vicky Compton's gardens, had been the long walks he took to remote places on their land. Sometimes with one or more of the Compass Boys, including Sterling's little brother, Bryant. He'd enjoyed sharing those things about their surroundings, and they'd practiced making fires a bunch too. Skills every kid who lived out here should have.

Still, civilization would be a nice change. Maybe they could grab some dinner before heading back. If she would deign to speak to him. Or even look at him. And if he could rustle up a shirt. Takeout, eaten in her shop, just the two of them sounded pretty fine too.

They pulled around the back of the row of stores on Main Street, and she guided him to the service entrance of her shop. He was impressed with her security system and the cameras until he considered her Uncle Sawyer was Compass Pass's sheriff and her store was full of semiprecious stones and metal.

She ushered him inside and locked the door behind them.

"So do I get the official tour?" he asked, breaking their verbal standoff.

"Um. Sure." She seemed surprised that he gave a shit, which only twisted the knife in his gut a little more.

"This is the current space. We've got the stockroom back here, which is nothing flashy. My workstation is up front and then the retail area is past that. I've been wanting to expand for a while, take on some pricier projects for online markets or maybe do some traveling shows. I just signed the lease a couple weeks ago when the space next door became available. We've had the shop closed with all these damn fixtures in here, but I need to reopen soon if I'm going to afford double the rent." She shook her head. "Of course, my dad keeps paying the bill because he's been too busy to help me, and I think my family likes me around to take Vivi to the doctor during the day and stuff, but I'm not looking for a handout from my family."

"You've done this all on your own." It wasn't a question. He could tell she had built it from the ground up. And done a damn fine job. The shop sucked him in. Quirky yet stylish, the way she had stuff arranged was clever. It made several of her pieces jump out.

Glancing around at the jewelry near him, he spotted a half-dozen items that he admired. This was not stuff you'd find in a kiosk on the mall. No, her jewelry was original. Gorgeous. Like her.

"My mom would have loved this pin. Her name was Haiwee. It means Dove." He pointed to a bird on a silver branch with ruby eyes. The detailing in the feathers made it seem as if it were about to launch into the air.

"Honestly, it's one of my favorites too. Would you mind if I named it after her?" Sterling smiled as she sidled closer. She didn't flinch when their arms touched.

"That—that would mean a lot to me. Thank you."

Sterling nodded. "You're welcome."

The more he looked, the more he realized she wasn't that different from him. She saw nature in a way most people didn't. A bracelet formed from a curve of wire dotted with blue crystal reminded him of a half-frozen stream.

All of her designs were exquisite. To his untrained eye, anyway.

"Wow, Sterling, you're fucking great at this. This one here, it's the sun, right? On a hazy day when you can see the heat waves." He turned toward her but couldn't see her eyes through the veil of her hair. So he reached out and tucked it behind her ear before he could think better of it.

"Yes." She smiled. "And thank you. Lots of people tell me my stuff is pretty, but no one ever seems to see what I do."

"Like this tree, with the leaves falling softly around it like they do after the first frost?" He pointed to a necklace with tiny emeralds dangling from dainty chains that forked off a roughly rectangular garnet.

"Exactly." She stared at him as if he'd somehow cheated on a test where no one knew the answers except her.

Sterling leaned toward him, but when she got too close, she jerked away as if singed by the heat smoldering between them. "Come on. We need to lug these cases into the other room and hook up the specialty lighting units. It's going to be a pain in the ass."

"Sounds like fun." As long as he got to do it with her.

Two hours later, he realized she hadn't been kidding. Sweat beaded on his bare chest as he connected the final wires with his aching finger. "There. Done."

He squirmed out from beneath the case and sat, resting his back against the wall. Sterling handed him a bottle of water, which he chugged. When he recapped the empty container, he caught her staring at him.

"What?" He wiped his mouth, self-conscious.

"Don't take this the wrong way, Viho, but I'm kind of glad you sliced yourself open before. You look pretty damn hot working without your shirt on."

Sterling ate up the plane of his chest—and his six-pack—with her hungry stare. "I think we should agree that you'll go shirtless from now on so we don't have to keep sabotaging your poor wardrobe."

He laughed, though it was hard to maintain his distance when their easy camaraderie extended beyond manual labor.

"You know, Vivi was right. You have the most amazing eyes." Sterling smiled as she touched his cheek. Innocently enough, despite his cock taking her stroke completely out of context. "Even Jake's aren't as bright gold as yours, though."

He turned away sharply.

"Why do you do that?" She tossed up her hands in frustration. "I don't understand you, Viho. One minute you're running hot. Then the next…this."

"There are things you don't understand, Sterling." He sighed as he climbed to his feet.

"Damn straight. Because you won't fucking tell me what's going on with you." She propped her hands on her hips. "What's your deal? Before you knew who I was, everything was…phenomenal between us. But the minute you found out that I was a Compass Girl, things changed. I don't get it."

"Used to everyone bowing down at your Compton feet?" he snarled.

"That." She pointed then approached until she poked him in the chest. "I don't get that attitude. What the hell has my family done to you? Answer me."

He clamped his jaw to keep from spilling everything. The past few hours in her company had made him weak. He truly admired her and wished he could share.

"You know what? If we're so awful, get the hell out. I'll loan you the money for a new truck and you can be on your way right now. Today." Her tapping toe warned him that her temper was about to blow.

Yet, somehow, the thought of leaving this town and the people he'd met—most of all her—didn't thrill him. In fact, it made him feel sick.

So maybe he owed it to her to be honest as she'd been with him from the start. He wanted to trust her.

Beyond stupid.

Still tempting.

"Tell me, Viho. What's going on?" This time she didn't screech. She snuck right in below his radar and his tensed arms to hug him, nuzzling his chest with her cheek.

There was no way he could fight that.

"Fine. You want to know all my secrets? How about this? Earlier, in the garden, your grandmother was closer than you realize. My damn eyes? The reason they look like his is because Jake is my father."

He couldn't believe he'd said it out loud.

Least of all to her.

Shit!

Of all the reactions she could have had, Viho never expected Sterling to bust out laughing. "You dickhead. I thought you were really going to let me in for a second. You suck."

He didn't move a muscle.

She didn't believe him?

He stared down at her, about to stride from the room and never look back.

Something in his face must have clued her in. She froze too. Then started talking at lightning speed, her voice pitched a full octave higher. "Oh my God, Viho. You're not joking, are you?"

He shook his head.

"Does Jake know?" She looked horrified. "He doesn't, does he?"

Viho shrugged. "My mom always swore he

didn't, but I didn't believe her. And now she's dead, so I can't exactly revisit the subject."

"I'm so sorry, Viho." She hugged him, then canted her head as she tried to make sense of the impossible. "So if you came here to find him, why haven't you told him who you really are?"

"Whoa. Hang on. I didn't do this on purpose. Hell, I was trying to stay far away. That's why I wasn't on the main road to start with. Except the engine locked up and…well, you know the rest." He couldn't help himself—Viho gathered Sterling into his arms and held her. It soothed him to have her close. No matter what happened now, at least he didn't have to carry his burden alone.

Sterling seemed content there, rubbing his back and hugging him in return.

He finally had his secret out in the open and the world hadn't ended.

Yet.

"I can't believe this," she whispered. "I promise I won't say anything, but, Viho, I think you should tell him. He would want to know."

"He never came for me. All those years. It would be awkward. He chose not to be part of my life. Who am I to make him pick differently now?" Viho hated the rasp in his voice.

"I get that he's your father, but I *know* Jake. He would never have given up the chance to have a family of his own. My mom tells stories…" Sterling cut off.

"Yes?" Viho had to learn more.

"Uh, this is kind of weird." She snorted. "Hate to break it to you, but your dad and my mom used to get it on."

"What?" He pulled back enough to catch her wry grin.

"Yep. Wild monkey sex, I'm pretty sure. It's not

like I asked for details, but there's a crap ton of winking and nudging going on between my aunts when they talk about it." She shook her head as if to clear it of the thoughts. "Remember, I told you Jake worked on the ranch before my dad came back from New York? Our parents kept each other company. Your dad has always seemed a little…broken. Distant. Now I think I know why. I still don't believe he knows you exist, but I bet he loved your mom something fierce."

"Oh yeah, so much that he forgot all about her and screwed your mom a bunch instead of chasing after my mom?" He didn't mean to hurt Sterling, but she flinched as though he'd slapped her. Before he could apologize, she countered.

With logic and something more primal.

"Are you saying you can't understand using sex to make yourself feel better?" she whispered as she kissed the side of his neck. Simultaneously, her hand snuck to his crotch and began to massage his limp cock, which responded to her manipulation despite the potent turmoil churning inside him. Maybe more because of it. "Don't lie to me, Viho. Who do you think it was you fucked that day in the middle of nowhere? How can we blame our parents when we both did the same thing?"

He made some non-distinct sound. It was the best he could do when she scraped her teeth over his jaw.

"In fact, I'd like to do it again. Right now. You know, in case you've forgotten how cathartic it is." She unfastened his pants, dipping her fingers beneath the waistband of his underwear to tease the lightly furred skin beneath. "I want to take away your pain. Or at least distract you from it."

Somehow he was sure she didn't mean the throbbing in his cut finger, which escalated in sync with his rising blood pressure.

"How can you?" he asked as he allowed himself

to run his fingers through her hair. She was right—the gesture did make him feel better. Less lonely.

"By making love to you right here, right now?" Standing on her tiptoes, she kissed him softly. Making him sip from her lips for another taste of her sweetness.

"Not that." He chuckled despite the situation, which should have made him want to cry instead. "I meant, how can you care? I've been such an asshole to you these past weeks."

"I forgive you." She kissed him again, then said, "I can see how hard this has been for you. I'm sure I would have acted like an idiot too if I were in your shoes."

Viho flat out laughed this time. Then he groaned. "I'm so much older than you. I'm thirty-eight, Sterling. Doesn't it bother you that I'm obviously a perv for going after someone not much more than half my age?"

"Nope. I don't care one bit. Did you know my grandfather JD was almost twenty years older than Vivi? People around here still talk about how epic their relationship was." She steeled her spine. He adored the determination in her eyes. Almost enough to raise more objections just so she could overcome them.

"Do you have a family anecdote for everything?" He nipped her lip.

"Probably. You could try me." She shrugged. "Or you could let it go and fuck me instead. I'm definitely in favor of the latter."

"Wait." He put his hand on her throat when she would have dipped in for another kiss. Because soon he wasn't going to be able to stop himself from accepting her offer. But he had to get one thing straight first.

"Viho—" She narrowed her eyes at him.

"Seriously, Sterling. You have to think this through. I'm not planning on hanging around. I just need to save up some more for my truck, and in the spring…I'm leaving." He didn't want to hurt her any more than he already had. So he was honest. "It's better if we don't get attached."

"I'm afraid it's too late for that." She bowled him over with the raw emotion in her eyes. "I've wanted you from the first instant I saw you. And now that I know what you're really made of, I admire you, Viho. I respect you. I want you. For however long I can have you."

"Are you certain?" He could only give her one more chance.

She didn't take it.

"Yes." Sterling Compton dropped to her knees in front of him. His head fell back as she finished undoing his jeans, then shoved them down. Grateful for the brown paper taped to the windows of the unopened storefront, he let her have her way.

Soon, she had his cock out and ready, her delicate fingers pumping slow but steady until he was fully erect. The instant her lips fastened around the head of his dick, he reflexively thrust his hips, filling her mouth with his arousal.

She didn't seem to mind, hungrily sucking on him as her fingers wandered lower, to tease his balls.

Viho was glad now not to have a shirt. It saved him some time. He kicked off his boots and jeans, then sank to the floor on top of Sterling. When they were both horizontal, he flipped around, never allowing his cock to leave her moist, warm, sucking—oh, God—mouth.

Once he situated himself, he immediately went to work peeling her jeans and pretty panties down her legs so that he could return the favor. Thankfully, she didn't try to stop him.

He hummed when he scented her arousal, spicy and delicious. Nothing could have prepared him for how good she tasted when he buried his mouth in her damp folds and licked.

Sterling shuddered beneath him and sucked harder. Deeper.

He took that as a good sign.

So he nuzzled her as he curled one finger, inserting it the barest bit inside her as he continued to breathe softly over her blushing flesh. Viho lapped at her, enjoying her squeals and sighs. He explored, discovering the spots she liked being touched best. What kind of pressure made her moan? He practiced the fluttering of his tongue that she preferred.

He could have eaten her for hours.

Except it wasn't long before she began to tremble in his arms. Her sucking grew careless and she caught his cock with the sharp edge of one of her teeth. He didn't mind, because he knew she was lost in the moment and the pleasure he was giving her.

His finger swept in and out of her at an even pace now, while he sucked on her clit with three short bursts of pressure before repeating the pattern.

"Mmmph!" She tried to warn him, but he didn't require notice.

Then she shoved at his hips, as if asking him to stop. No way would he fall short of granting her the ultimate pleasure. Hell no. She would come on his face. Then he'd make her do it again while he fucked her. There was no reason she couldn't have both.

Her pussy clamped around his finger, squeezing in rhythmic pulses that matched her moans. He grinned as she unraveled, her orgasm spectacular and prolonged. And when she calmed, he withdrew his cock from her still suckling mouth, sighing at the loss of pressure, though he knew it was only temporary.

Then he spun to face her, eye to eye. He kissed her glistening lips in thanks, then beamed down at her.

"Go ahead and be proud of yourself." She shot him a lazy smile. "You're pretty damn good at that."

"Thanks. And I think you'll be glad to know I did manage to bum a ride to the clinic. We're good to go on the Vasalgel." He raised his brows at her and she smiled, wiping the corner of her mouth on her knuckles. He'd never seen something so sexy in his whole life.

"I *am* happy to hear that." She grinned, then rolled him to his back, not bothering to take more time to recover from her epic release.

Viho surrendered, letting her have control since he'd jerked her around for weeks. She deserved to take the reins. And he'd willingly follow.

When her fingers encircled his shaft, he shuddered then waited, mostly patient, for her to introduce the bulging head of his cock to her pussy. He licked his lips, savoring the taste of her honey even as she slathered his erection in it, making him slide deep inside her on the very first stroke.

"Damn," he groaned and pounded the floor with his fist. He thrust upward, reaching deeper inside her, but she lifted off.

"Oh, come on, Viho." She *tsked* at him, schoolmarm style, making him harder than even before. "Not so fast. You made me wait more than a month for this. Let's make it last."

Except someone should tell her that rolling her hips like that was not the way to boost a man's endurance. It wouldn't be him. He simply enjoyed it, his hands landing on her waist to help support her while she rode him with fluid glides.

"Easy to say that when you've just had what looked to be a fan-*fucking*-tastic orgasm," he huffed.

"It was. Thank you," she added primly, making him laugh.

Sex, amusement and comfort. What more could

he want from a partner?

"You're welcome." Viho moaned when she dropped all the way down on his shaft, connecting them fully. She ground against his body, rubbing her clit on him as she did something wicked with the muscles inside her pussy, which massaged him exactly right.

"Fuck!"

"Since you asked so nicely." She chuckled at the mock-outrage on his face, then gave him what he'd asked for. Riding him, she filled herself with his erection and ushered him deep inside her at the same time. Her palms splayed on his chest, making him feel less self-conscious about his size. Useful. Good for supporting her. Protecting her.

The thought alone had him hovering on the edge of orgasm.

Sterling froze.

"What?" He couldn't be more eloquent at the moment.

"Did you think I was kidding about making you wait?" She traced his lips with the tip of one finger, humming when he parted to suck her inside and nibble on the digit.

"Hmm?"

"You're cute when you're horny." She grinned. "I'm not letting you come yet. Maybe not for a while."

"Sterling!" He could have rolled over and hammered into her, coming in a moment. But where was the fun in that? Maybe she was on to something.

So he played her game.

Besides, he liked that despite his advantages—in size, strength and age—she wasn't afraid to put him in his place.

Viho reached up and palmed her taut breasts. He savored the weight of them in his hands, the rasp of her nipples jabbing in the center. When he brushed his thumbs over the peaks, she arched, planting her hands on his thighs to give him better access. She gasped, her breasts more sensitive than any woman's he'd ever had the honor of touching.

She also rocked over him involuntarily, granting him a moment of relief that soon became tension. He could come so easily in her. She fit him perfectly.

He trailed his fingers down her softly rounded stomach to her pussy, then gave her clit similar treatment. While he teased her, she began to fuck him harder and deeper again, rewarding his attention.

Her thighs began to tremble around him and he knew she wouldn't be able to deny him for much longer. Except just then, she stopped again.

"Ugh." He let his head fall backward onto the plank flooring.

"Viho, tell me you want this. That you want me." For a change, her plea seemed timid and when he peeked into her eyes, they were glassy.

Ah, shit. He had hurt her with his callous treatment. He knew he had.

"I do. Can you feel me, Sterling? I've never been this hard for a woman in all my life. Let me fuck you." It wasn't really a request as he held her hips still and began to drive upward into her from below. "Let me show you how much I need this."

She stared into his eyes as he let go, allowing himself to take everything she offered and give all of himself in return. He made sure to swivel his hips, keeping up the pressure on her clit as she'd shown him she preferred when she'd done the work, rubbing herself on him. He plowed into her, slapping them together as she tightened impossibly around him.

And when she screamed his name, he didn't have to be told she was coming.

She drew the seed straight from his balls and

filled herself as she sucked pump after pump from him with the matched spasms of her pussy. He emptied into her with a roar.

Never before had he felt so accepted.

So at home.

Shit.

Viho closed his eyes to block out the thought as he cradled Sterling on his chest so she didn't have to lie on the cold, hard floor. He held her as she began to shake and sobs bubbled from her chest.

"I'm sorry. So sorry I hurt you." He thought of the weeks he'd mandated their separation. Of how he'd lied by omission. Foolish to deny them both this connection.

"Crying *for* you. For Jake." She sniffled. "Your mom. It's not fair."

And suddenly Viho wished he could join her.

Instead, he let Sterling bawl for all the nights he'd spent alone.

A single tear tracked down his cheek as he traced circles on her back, impressed with her sensitivity and empathy. Since when had anyone cared about his suffering?

Sterling Compton was special, and she deserved the best from him.

From life.

Which probably meant going on without him.

Chapter Seven

Sterling couldn't believe it was so late. She stared at the kitchen clock as she ate some toast, still in her bathrobe and fuzzy slippers.

True, she and Viho had worked their asses off the day before, reorganizing the shop, then piled on to their exhaustion with some more enjoyable physical exertion, but still, she'd never slept past noon in her life. Not even as a teenager.

Certainly never until three o'clock in the afternoon.

She wondered if something was wrong with her. Maybe her mom had been right. She'd felt like she had the flu on and off for almost ten days. She figured that must be why she hadn't gotten her period yet either. A trip to the doctor might not be a terrible idea.

She sniffled, hoping it passed soon so she could get back to normal.

Hopefully she didn't make Viho sick either. She'd felt fine yesterday. Amazing, actually.

And that was when Hope wandered in. Her cousin worked some odd hours depending on what shift she had at the pharmacy. Today she probably had a graveyard scheduled.

"What's going on?" Hope rested her hip on the

kitchen counter. Although she lived with Wyatt and Clay now, she still kept a few things in her old bedroom since the Compass Girl cabin had a hell of a lot more square footage than the place she shared with her men. Probably came by to collect some stuff or check on Sterling when she hadn't shown up at the main house all day. At least it wasn't her dad or mom who had dropped in.

This would be a lot harder to explain if they had.

"I slept with Viho again yesterday." Sterling figured there was no sense in lying.

"And it wasn't as good as the first time?" Hope frowned. "I really thought the two of you would make an awesome couple."

"No, no. That's not it. It was great. I want more from him, but he's not into it. Not planning to stick around after he finishes Vivi's garden." She shrugged. "That's part of why he was staying away from me. He didn't want either of us to get attached when it can't end well."

"I guess that plan backfired, now didn't it?"

"Yup." Sterling sniffled again. "And I swear to God I don't know what's wrong with me. I feel crappy. Everything is making me cry. Hell, I broke down after we came yesterday. I'm not that kind of girl—the weepy-after-sex kind. You know I'm not. The only person less likely to turn on the waterworks after a damn fine orgasm than me is Jade."

"Yeah, but she's different around Liam. Maybe you're not the same with Viho." Hope sat beside her.

"I guess." Sterling's shoulders slumped.

"Or... You told me you were late on your period last week. Have you still not gotten it?"

"Stop right there, Hope. You've got freaking babies on the brain lately. Don't aim that nonsense this way." Sterling put her arms up in a big X, as if warding off an evil creature.

"You're right. I'm pretty much obsessed. I've been reading everything I can. You know we're not waiting until the wedding to try. So don't you think I know the signs?" Hope didn't hesitate. With surprising strength, she grabbed Sterling and yanked her to her feet. "I have a whole case of tests stashed in the bathroom. What would it hurt—?"

"No." Sterling tried to dig in her heels, but she was too tired to win.

"Viho was at the end of his Vasalgel, right?" Why did her lunatic cousin seem excited when this was horrifying enough to make Sterling want to stick her head under the pillows and conk out again? For a week this time.

"Stop. Hope, seriously. This isn't funny."

"No, it's not. If you're pregnant you need to—"

"Gah! Don't say that like it could be real." Sterling stuffed her fingers in her ears.

"It *could* be." They marched down the hall, then Hope tossed a cardboard box at Sterling. "Pee on it. Pronto."

She slammed the bathroom door.

Sterling looked at the box. She even read the directions on the insta-test.

"You're not getting out of there until you do it." Hope sing-songed, surely barricading the bathroom door. Sterling could usually take her, but not feeling like this, she couldn't.

"Fuck you. Fine." It was easier than fighting over something so stupid anyway.

She did the deed, cleaned up, set the test on the sink, then flung open the door.

Hope perched on the other side, nibbling her lip, as if there was anything to worry about.

"Would you quit that? I am *not* pregnant."

Sterling picked up the test and shoved it in her cousin's face. "Read it yourself."

"Sterling..." Hope sounded like she might pass out. Or cry herself. Or shriek.

"What?" she shouted.

"You're having a baby."

"That's not funny." Sterling rolled her eyes. "Don't fuck around about something like that."

"You know I wouldn't." Hope reached out, honesty in her eyes. "I've prayed for that result so many times lately. You're lucky, Sterling. You're going to be a mom."

Her dizziness amplified as she snatched the test back and looked at it. Then did a double take. And next thing she knew, she was crashing to the floor.

Funny, she'd never known what it felt like to faint before.

A day of firsts.

Sterling came to with Hope crouched next to her, shaking her awake while on the phone. She'd called the other two Compass Girls. Probably to get medical advice from Sienna before ordering them to meet up at the main house as soon as possible.

"What are you doing?" Sterling felt queasy.

"We're going to talk to Vivi." Hope swallowed hard. "She'll know what to do, the right things to say, and she won't remember we told her so she can't slip up and tell our parents before you're ready."

"I can't believe this just happened." Sterling climbed to her feet in a daze. She clung to Hope as they piled into the car and made the quick trip over to the main house.

By the time they arrived, Jade and Sienna waited on the front porch. Sterling hustled inside quickly, afraid of seeing Viho, if he worked outside. How would she tell him? Should she? He'd made it clear that he planned to leave.

Oh God.

She whimpered.

"Shh." Hope held her hand as they snuck inside. "It's going to be okay."

"You can't know that." Sterling barely made it inside before she collapsed into a dining room chair and began sobbing.

"Oh, my!" Vivi raced, as quickly as she could, around the table and hugged Sterling. "What's wrong, dear?"

Sterling wasn't sure her grandmother knew which of the Compass Girls she was, or maybe she might even have thought she was one of the Mothers instead, but her comfort was universal. And greatly appreciated.

For long minutes, she tried to spit out the problem, but each time she opened her mouth more blubbering spilled out. Surrounded by her cousins and grandmother, she knew she was safe to express her shock and grief. This wasn't what she had planned for herself.

Kids had never been on her radar.

But that didn't mean she hadn't wanted any. Just that she hadn't thought about it. Didn't figure she was ready.

When she'd managed to suppress the flood, limiting the proof of her breakdown to intermittent hiccups, Sterling said, "I'm pregnant."

"What?" Jade stood up so fast, her chair tipped over and crashed to the floor.

"I know." Her shoulders slumped. "I can't believe I let this happen."

Her cousin tried to backpedal. "No, no. It's just a shock, that's all."

"Congratulations." Vivi beamed as she clasped

her hands in front of her. "This is such a great day, Sterling. For you and…"

She grew quiet.

"I don't remember who your husband is." For the first time, Vivi seemed defeated. "I'm sorry."

Sterling couldn't take any more heartache. She dropped her head on her crossed arms on the table and mumbled, "I'm not married."

"Oh, well, then I don't feel so bad." Vivi giggled. "Is that why you're upset over such fantastic news?"

"It's not how I imagined my life." Sterling winged her watery gaze to Sienna and Jade, who seemed to be recovering.

"Do you think this is how I pictured mine?" Vivi shrugged. "Sometimes we have to cope with what we're dealt. Gracefully. And trust me, you've been given a gift."

Sterling couldn't imagine it in those terms just yet. Because surely, this would mean the end of her budding relationship with Viho. Either he was going to be furious, since he planned to head out, or he'd cling, because of his own upbringing. Not because of her.

"Maybe we have." She looked to Hope. "Why can't I be a surrogate for you, Wy and Clay? You want a baby. Right?"

Hope's mouth opened then closed so many times she looked like a fish out of water.

"I—" More cut off sentences and random sounds followed as her cousin sputtered.

"This baby of yours will be loved by our family one way or another. It will live a life full of joy and some sadness. That's the way it is and always will be." Vivi put her hand on Sterling's stomach. "There's no need to make big decisions today. There's plenty of time for that. You know, I remember when I found out about each of you kids. And your brothers. Hope especially, since your mom told JD the good news hours before he died. It was the last secret he shared with me."

In the quiet that followed, Sterling distantly heard a creak, but she dismissed it as Vivi settled into the seat near her. Old houses made lots of those noises.

"That's the thing. This *has* to stay secret." Sterling's mind raced. She imagined the coming months. "Viho can't know. You guys don't understand how fucked up this is."

"So tell us." Sienna held her hand. "We're here for you. We'll do whatever it takes to help out."

"Viho didn't mean to come here. You know, he broke down. He's not staying. He was very clear about that. I can't force him to change his plans by tying him to me like this." She swiped endless tears from her cheeks as she realized how much he would hate her if he knew.

And how much more he would hate her if he didn't.

"It's not right to keep this miracle from the baby's father." Vivi was stern. "It's his obligation, and his *right*, to be a part of this baby's life."

"Oh God, if you only knew." Sterling rocked herself, unraveling again. "He would never forgive me. He's torn up inside because his own dad isn't in the picture. Never has been."

Even in her misery and despair, she vowed to keep the pertinent details secret. "He told me about it last night. That his mom fell in love with a rancher. But for some reason, she didn't tell the guy that she'd gotten pregnant. She felt an obligation to her family. They sound a little out there, obsessed with outdated customs. And I think they pressured her about her lineage. I guess forty years ago things could have been different too. She was young and had been raised to think like them, you know? So she caved and went back to the reservation. The problem was, some of the people there didn't approve of her non-traditional relationship. She was ostracized. Viho too. They were kind of outcasts. At least when he was growing up. So when his mom passed away, he walked. Didn't want any part of that nonsense. And who could blame him? He didn't have what we have, you know? A big family. All this love. I could never betray him like that…to not tell him about his own child…"

"What is his mother's name?" Oak chair legs scrapped the floor as Sterling and her cousins spun to face Jake, who'd asked the question in an eerie and ominous rasp. His ashen face glowed in the late afternoon sunlight as the fresh flowers he'd obviously brought in for Vivi fell from his limp fingers.

Sterling thought she might black out again.

"Tell me!" he roared as he crossed the floor with three strides. He shook Sterling, hard. "What is Viho's mother's name? Is it Haiwee? Where is she? Tell me, Sterling. Tell me now!"

"What the fuck is going on here?" Sam bellowed right back. He and Cindi, like always, weren't far behind Jake. Sterling's father took one look at the fear in her eyes and mistook it. She could never really be afraid of Jake. No, she was terrified of hurting him. "Why do you have your hands on my daughter? What is this about?"

"Oh fucknuggets," Hope, who rarely swore, cursed beneath her breath.

Sterling almost broke out in hysterics.

"Is it true, Sterling?" Jake trembled where his hands fisted in her shirt. "Am *I* the sucker you were just talking about, who never got to know his family? Is Viho my son?"

Cindi gasped. She raced to Jake and hugged him

from behind.

One by one, Sam pried Jake's fingers from Sterling.

"Yes." The man in question stood in the door. Tall and handsome, he stared at her as if she were scum. "Sterling hasn't lied. I believe you are my father."

Sterling wobbled as she got to her feet and crossed the room. She reached out to Viho, but he shoved her away. She tripped, skidding across the polished wood floor, hugging her stomach.

"Stop this!" Hope draped over her, shielding her. She glared at Viho. "You may hate her right now, but don't fuck up too badly or you'll never know your own child. Don't hurt the mother of your baby."

"Excuse me?" Sam whipped around from where he'd braced Jake, either to keep him from rampaging or crushing Viho in a hug; Sterling had no idea at this point.

"Sterling?" Cindi's eyes were wide and her mouth hung open at the chaos around them all.

Sterling crawled out of the midst of the insanity, then clung to the doorframe as she found her feet. A room full of Comptons had never managed to be so quiet. Until now.

Good thing too because she could hardly manage a sarcastic whisper. "Yes, I'm knocked up. Hooray."

When it seemed like everyone in the room would rush her, except Viho, who might as well have been turned to stone for all he moved, Vivi headed them off. She stepped in between Sterling and the rest of the commotion. "You will leave her alone. Let her think. Everyone calm down. This is not how I raised my family to behave. Sit your asses down. All of you."

Even Sterling took a step forward, but Vivi shook her head. "I think you should go outside and get some air. The barn has a good track record for helping people think things through."

Dazed, Sterling nodded.

She dodged Viho without meeting his stare and bolted before anyone could stop her.

Chapter Eight

"Why don't you come in, Viho?" Cindi Compton reached out to him, drawing him into their nest. He'd never felt so out of place in his life. Not even on the reservation, where he knew people feared him and what his leadership could mean to their conservative ways, though he never planned to stake any claim. That was why he'd left.

"I don't think that's a good idea." He shook his head, keeping his feet planted.

"What the hell were you doing here?" Jake stood, his fists balled.

"I heard shouting. I thought something might be wrong with Sterling. Or Mrs. Compton." He blinked, speaking as mechanically as a robot. Was this really happening?

"Did you come to Compass Ranch to extort me? Or to make me pay by hurting Sterling? Because I've treated her like my own daughter when I thought…" Jake swallowed hard.

"What?" Viho rocked onto his heels. The last of his childish hopes for a cheerful reunion smashed as surely as the blooms scattered on the floor. His own father thought so little of him. He supposed he'd given the guy no reason to think otherwise. "I wouldn't—"

"Jake," Sam Compton barked at his friend, grabbing the guy's arm. "Think about what you're saying. This isn't you."

"Where is she?" Jake pressed on as if he hadn't heard the sage advice.

"Sterling?" Viho could hardly think of anyone else. She was pregnant? Right now. With his child? She'd looked so scared. Horrified, actually.

"No. Your mother. Where is Haiwee?" Jake leaned forward, straining the limits of Sam Compton's strength as he snarled.

More sadness piled on Viho's shoulders. They were ox-like, but they could only take so much. This might be his limit. "Gone. Dead. Two months ago. Cancer."

"No!" Jake howled. He smashed his fists into the table repeatedly. "No."

The longer Viho stood there, watching the surreal scene in front of him, the angrier he got. At the selfish man he no longer cared much about knowing. At the woman he'd respected and duped himself into thinking he might be falling for—or could, if he stuck around.

All his life he'd worked on keeping his temper in check, knowing people mistrusted him simply because of who he was and how overgrown he was. His mother had drummed the importance of control into him. For the first time ever, he felt that composure cracking.

"I can't believe she told you my secret." Viho shook his head. Obviously Sterling's loyalties didn't lie with him. Their connection, false. "And that she didn't share with me about the baby."

He figured he hadn't given her much chance over the past month, when he'd ignored her. But last night...why hadn't she confided in him then?

It seemed like her family was about to make a shit ton of excuses and he didn't give a fuck about any of them. They'd almost conned him into thinking they weren't the greedy people he'd always imagined, stealing his father when they had plenty of family of their own in their ridiculous Compass clan.

Several breaths huffed out of him as he prepared to unleash his rage. Bottled for so long, the resounding explosion would be epic.

Except, just then, Sterling's mom approached. Unafraid of his flaring nostrils or the maroon tint to his skin, she ignored Sam's call and reached out. Not in anger, or shock, or fear, but in acceptance.

"Give her a chance to explain." Cindi hugged Viho. "I'm not saying my daughter is perfect, but I know her heart. She would never so cruelly betray someone she cares for. Like it or not, Viho, you're part of this family. Forever bound. Twice over. I promise you we will make you proud of that one day."

They wanted to impress *him*? Viho's eyes stung as he looked around the room.

Sterling's cousins nodded, smiling.

He thought of how they'd pushed Sterling toward him the day before.

And at the head of the table, Mrs. Compton wept. She held Jake's hand in one of hers and reached to Viho with the other. "Come here."

She wasn't the kind of woman you said no to.

So he didn't.

"Please forgive him." Vicky Compton took Viho's fingers, as much of them as she could grip. From beside them, sloppy sobs echoed from Viho's father. He wailed for Haiwee, but Viho could have assured him that she could no longer hear either of their desperate pleas. "Jake has never gotten over your mom. He couldn't understand why she left. He never knew what he'd done to make her run from him. I'm sorry. He's a better man than this, I swear. *You* are too. My granddaughter needs you. Please. Go to her. Stop this chain of ugliness. It only takes one person to begin turning things around. You can make this right. Please, do it."

Viho felt his betrayal, rage and—most of all—fear melt from him as he stared into Vicky Compton's clear blue eyes. This was the most lucid he'd ever seen her. When her family needed her, she fought for them. *That* was what he wanted. She was right. He had the power to avoid the mistakes his own parents had made. He had to be responsible now.

Not for himself.

But for his child.

Who would never know the pain he had endured if he could help it.

Without a backward glance at his father, he left the house, stumbling down the stairs then jogging across the yard. By the time he reached the barn doors, he was sprinting full out.

Toward his future.

"Sterling?" Viho slowed in time to avoid crashing through the door like a cartoon, leaving a man-shaped cutout in his wake. He didn't want to scare her or seem aggressive. Not after the commotion in the main house.

She didn't respond.

Instead, Wyatt stood barely inside, poking furiously at his phone. He glanced up at Viho. "What the hell is going on?"

"Have you seen Sterling? I need to talk to her." He didn't have time to explain.

"Yeah, I saw her. She's huddled in the corner of one of the empty stalls, crying her eyes out. I cleared the rest of the guys out of here so she could have some privacy." He glared at Viho. "Clay's trying to calm her down. And Hope isn't answering my texts. Did you do this?"

"You could say that." He deflated. "Look, the shit just hit the fan up in the main house. You guys are going to want to head over there. I'll take care of Sterling. I promise."

"I think I'd rather wait to hear from Hope." When Wyatt didn't seem like he planned to budge anytime soon, Viho dropped his bomb.

"It can't be good for a pregnant woman to be so upset. If anything happens to her, it's on you. And I'm not going to take kindly to some asshole hurting my family." He rose up to his full height.

"Did you say—?"

"Yes. Move. *Now*." Viho smiled wolfishly when Wy stepped aside. "Thank you for looking out for her."

"Anytime." The other guy's eyes were huge in the dim interior of the barn. "Clayton, let's go."

He seemed like he might have argued, but when he turned and saw Viho coming, he stopped cooing in mid-sentence, grabbed his hat and left the unlikely pair to their private matters, murmuring as he passed, "Good luck, Chief."

Viho nodded, then ducked into the stall. He held his breath at the rush of emotions that slammed into him when he saw Sterling. He tamped down the negative ones and tried to magnify the positive—protection, awe, pride and affection.

Before wrecking the moment by opening his giant mouth and stuffing his boot in, he settled beside her and opened his arms. Sterling surprised him when she flew into them, crashing against his chest. She shook like a shoot in a tornado, scaring him with the intensity of her response.

"Hey now. It's going to be okay." He tried every trick he knew to soothe her. Petting her hair, rubbing her back, rocking her gently, promising things he couldn't be sure were true. "We'll find a way to make this work."

A long time passed, filled with nothing but those reassuring whispers. And then, finally, an enormous, shaky breath from the woman in his arms. She relaxed against him and hugged him back.

"I'm so sorry, Viho." She crumpled his shirt in her hands as she clung to him. "That was…a disaster."

He had so many things to ask her. Starting with, how could you tell them my secret?

But he didn't.

As if she could read his mind, she answered him anyway. "I can't believe this is real. That everything went down like that. I swear, Viho, I didn't tell Jake who you were. I didn't keep this baby from you."

She rushed to explain herself. So he let her.

"I didn't know. I promise. I haven't been feeling so good. And sure, I was late, but I figured it was because I've been kind of sick. Then I was so tired today. I blew it off thinking…well, you know…that yesterday wore me out." A weak laugh left her, making Viho take a deep breath for the first time in what seemed like ten years. "I didn't even suspect. So dumb of me. Hope made me take the test."

"So you've only known for a little bit yourself?" He hugged her tighter.

"An hour, I guess," she confirmed.

"Oh, Sterling." A portion of his resentment evaporated. "You're still coming to terms with this too?"

"I don't think I've even started, Viho." She looked up at him with diamond tears dangling from her lashes. They made her look heartbreakingly beautiful, more even than if they'd been some of her exquisite jewelry. "I went to see Vivi, get her advice and deal with the news. I told them—"

Her story faltered as her anxiety ratcheted up

again.

"Shhh." He stroked his palms up and down her arms. "It's okay that you shared my past. Under these circumstances. Well, you were shocked—"

"I didn't." Sterling stiffened in his grasp. "I swear, Viho. I didn't tell them about Jake."

"Well, he certainly knew by the time I heard the ruckus and showed up." This time it was her soothing him with hugs and kisses on his neck that were surprisingly effective.

"I was irrational. Still probably am. Freaking out. This isn't how I'd planned for my life to turn out, you know?" She pleaded him to understand with big, soft doe eyes that he couldn't resist.

"Yeah, I think I can relate." He smiled a bit.

"I started to talk crazy about giving up the baby to Hope, Wy and Clay. They're trying you know?" As soon as the confession left her lips, he froze, though he tried to stay open-minded. "And then I realized how unfair that was to you. And that given the situation, you'd never have a child without being involved in their life."

"Damn straight," he growled.

"I told them how you were raised. I think Jake must have been standing in the other room. He guessed. He asked what your mom's name was. I think, Viho, he must have had an inkling. Maybe you remind him of your mom, just like Vivi saw his eyes in you." She shivered. "He grabbed me and started yelling. Demanding to know the truth. I swear, I didn't tell him."

"No, *I* did." Viho rewound the horrible scene in his mind. Sterling hadn't crossed him after all.

"I know it's not what you wanted. None of this is." More tears leaked from her. "I'm so sorry. What are we going to do?"

"First, we're going to dry your eyes." He dabbed at her face. "This should be a happy occasion, Sterling."

"Really?" She peeked up at him. "You're not angry?"

"If I was, I'd only have myself to blame. I knew my prescription was running out. I should have stopped myself that day. But I couldn't. No, I didn't want to." He didn't glance away when he promised her, "I don't regret taking that risk, and I will accept responsibility for my actions. No matter what, this peanut did *nothing* wrong and I won't have its life start out with accusations and anger."

He laid his hand on her stomach and she clutched his fingers.

"We made something phenomenal. If we work together instead of against each other, we'll be better off in every way." He nuzzled her nose with his.

"Partners?" she asked.

"Partners." He liked the sound of that. Someone he could count on. A person he would look after. Well, two of them, he supposed. Tenderness swamped him when he watched Sterling and imagined her growing full and ripe with his child. He pictured her rocking a baby, swaddled in soft blankets.

It wasn't a bad vision at all. In fact, he groaned, never having imagined he'd have that kind of domestic tie in his life.

He couldn't guess what Sterling conjured as she stared right back at him, but it must have been something equally as inspiring because she leaned forward and rose up, seeking. Him.

This time when their lips met, it was like sealing a pact. They caressed each other with kindheartedness and consideration that seemed appropriate for a mate. Sweet, lingering contact spoke to Viho on an instinctual level that surpassed any vows they could exchange.

Finally, they broke apart, leaving a serene energy humming between them.

"I'm glad I'm in this with you," Sterling whispered.

And honestly, he couldn't think of another woman he would rather have for a partner. Though he hadn't known her long, she'd already surpassed any other lover he'd had in his estimation. Good thing, too, since they were bound for life.

"I'll try my best to never let you down." He kissed her softly. "Our baby either. I'm going to be the best dad I can be. And the best husband too."

"Huh?" Sterling jerked, plopping off his lap into the hay on the floor. "Who said anything about getting married? Viho, I hardly know you."

"Well enough to have a baby together." Could she seriously be balking after all they'd discussed. "What happened to *partners*?"

"That can mean a lot of things." She got to her feet and held out her hands. "Like my dad has partners in running the ranch. They're not *married*!"

"So I'm good enough to fuck, but not good enough to be legally yours?" Hurt rained over him as he realized if it weren't for the baby, she'd never have considered him more than tryst material. He'd wasted his breath the night before, warning her that he had planned to leave. She'd probably shrugged her shoulders mentally when he'd admitted that.

"No. I mean, I don't know. We've only known each other a little while." Sterling glanced over her shoulder, as if searching for an escape route.

He wasn't trying to trap her, but what other freedoms did she expect?

"Are you going to want to screw other guys? Bring them around our child? Use me, then leave me when you find Mr. Right instead of Mr. Side-of-the-

Road? Some guy who can treat my kid like he's not good enough because he's not genetically connected?" Viho knew he was losing it because of his own childhood, but he couldn't stop the pain from venting after all he'd endured. Right when he thought things were going okay, they always took a turn straight into the shitter.

He was tired of the stench.

"That's not what this is about, Viho." Sterling closed her eyes. "It's just that in my family, people marry for love. Not out of obligation. That level of commitment isn't a simple contract. It has to be more than that to last. We're not going to do this baby any good if we find out in a year or two that we made a mistake by rushing into things."

"A little too late to decide that, isn't it?" he growled.

"I'm going to cut you some slack, Viho." She stepped back once, then again, picking up speed. "I know what this must sound like to you. And we're both on edge right now. I think we should say goodnight. You can come over in the morning."

"If that's how you feel about things, I'm not sure I want to."

She flinched, but he didn't comfort her. Viho had been rejected one too many times in his life. He couldn't stand another.

So he watched as Sterling Compton, and his child, staggered out of his life.

Probably for good.

Chapter Nine

After several hours tossing and turning in his bunk, Viho gave up all pretense of sleep.

"Settle down, Chief. If you don't want to get some shuteye, would you mind leaving the rest of us to it? We gotta be up before dawn," one of the hands grumbled from the other side of the room.

At first, it'd irritated him that they called him the one thing he'd never wanted to be. Bad enough the elders on the reservation had insisted on it. It'd bugged him for about two seconds… Until he realized it was a sign of respect not a generalization, or worse, a slur. The guys around the ranch had come to him, asking him for advice when they realized he was a decent listener, with a calm mind, who'd keep his mouth shut. Either that or because he was twice as old as some of them. Maybe they figured that made him wiser. Either way, he'd kind of come to like it. For the first time, he felt measured on his own merit. A guy they looked to as a leader. Plus, it was a hell of a lot better than some of the nicknames the rest of the guys ended up with—Stumpy, Pony, Slicker or Deadwood to name a few.

"Sorry." Viho swung over the edge and dropped to the floor with a surprising amount of stealth given his size. He didn't bother to put his boots on before he wandered outside. Cold smacked him in his chest, making him curl inward against the fall night air. He ambled across the lawn to his truck, which he hadn't gotten rid of yet.

It might be a piece of shit, but it was all he had.

So he yanked open the door and climbed inside. He splayed, as much as he could, across the bench seat, flinging one arm over his face. The other dangled into the foot well, where it knocked against his duffle.

He'd kept some of his more personal stuff out here. Mostly because he didn't need it on a daily basis and the quarters were pretty cramped with the ranch hands' gear, but also because he didn't care to think of anyone poking around in his shit.

Hell, even he hadn't gone through all of his mom's stuff after she passed away.

Most of it he'd donated to charity. Clothes, dishes, utilitarian stuff like that.

But he'd kept the rare pictures she'd had. And her diary.

If ever there was a day he wished he could talk to her, it'd be this one. She'd have been thrilled to hear of a grandchild on the way, considering how often she'd nagged him about his loner tendencies and finding a decent girl to settle down with. She might not have picked Sterling from the crowd given her fierce independent streak, but she would have liked her once she'd gotten to know her.

Viho smiled in the darkness, then rummaged in the bag for the leather-bound book. In the process, a miniature turquoise figurine of a tortoise tumbled onto the plastic floor mat. Good luck, his mother had always said. He sure as hell could use some of that, so he pocketed the little guy before fishing through his meager belongings again.

Got it. He turned the fat, tattered volume over and

over in his hands. Just knowing his mom had held it, written in it for hours, days, years… It made him feel more connected to her spirit.

With a sigh, he reached up and flipped the truck's visor open, thankful the vehicle's battery still had some juice in it. The tiny makeup light provided barely enough illumination to read by when combined with the full moon and the host of stars twinkling in the Wyoming night sky.

From his quick perusal when he'd discovered the journal, he'd seen that the final entry in the book had come the day Haiwee returned to the reservation. Pregnant. With him.

Had she felt like he did when he'd gotten the news? Shocked, amazed, giddy and scared shitless wrapped into a ball of excitement?

Playing private-thought roulette, he flipped the pages, stopping randomly on one. Then he began to read.

Jake is by far the best lover I've ever had. When he touches me…

"Damn it! Mom!" Viho wrinkled his nose and skimmed a few pages more, peeking through half-closed eyes to avoid another glimpse into her sex life.

He figured the stuff he wanted to know most would be near the end, so he skipped ahead.

It's a hard choice. Love or security. Family or soul mate. Old traditions or new ones.

I honestly don't know what I'll do.

This baby deserves to grow up living his heritage. I owe it to my people—my parents—to continue doing things our way when the rest of the tribes are leaving those ways behind. Our community too. Getting more like the outside. Will this baby be happy without the skills our people can teach him? Like my father asked, how could he be? I haven't been gone long, but it's enough to see that the world is so very different out here. It's terrifying and huge sometimes. Easy to get lost. Like I feel now.

And Jake, my love. He would never survive away from ranching. This is what he was born to do. Is it fair to make him choose between this life and me?

Maybe it would be better for us all if I disappear.

Viho's stomach turned to lead.

Could she really have thought that would have been the correct answer to her questions? Hell, it's not like he'd grown up wealthy, or prized. Her family had looked down on her for running away, being disloyal. They'd made an example of Haiwee, sent her to live in a small bungalow on the outskirts of their land when they realized she'd returned home pregnant by an outsider.

They'd never deserved her loyalty.

So, then why hadn't she returned to Jake?

What had kept her there? Pride?

And what gave her the right to make decisions for Jake? If Sterling had done that to Viho…

He snapped the book shut, afraid to read any more and ruin the memories of the one person who had loved him unconditionally. But maybe his father wasn't the one to blame in all of this. People in tough situations didn't always think rationally. And though their hearts were in the right places, they still could fuck up royally.

Is that what he'd done tonight? By pushing Sterling?

Probably.

Unlike Haiwee, he was willing to admit his mistakes. To try to correct them. Tomorrow, he would make it up to Sterling and promise her that he would support their child, and her, in whatever form that took. However much of him she was willing to accept, that was what she would have.

The diary felt heavy where it rested on top of his heart.

Everything that had happened in the past twenty-four hours and the revelations he'd had about himself and his place in the universe exhausted him. He managed to doze for an hour or two until the sunlight sparkled through his cracked dash, rousing him. Time for work. At least he was good at that. Manual labor could be exactly the outlet he required to alleviate his frustration.

How could he make things right?

With Sterling.

With Jake.

With the memory of his mother. It was awfully hard to fight a ghost.

Especially one you wanted to hug instead.

Viho didn't regret his decision to tackle the removal of several stubborn stumps. It gave him a great excuse to hack at long-buried roots, venting the pent up emotions inside him. Wearing himself out more with every swing of the axe, he was drenched in sweat and cursing up a storm when someone called his name.

Jake.

He tossed the axe to the ground, then turned and plopped onto one of the chunks of wood he'd already excavated. Catching his breath, he stared up at the guy he wasn't sure he was ready to face.

Seemed he didn't have a choice.

His father glanced around awkwardly before asking, "Mind if I have a seat?"

"It's not very comfortable. But it's your ass."

Jake chuckled as he sat. He winced, then pulled a splinter from his jeans before tossing the offending sliver over his shoulder. "So…"

"So," Viho echoed as he nodded.

"I guess I first need to apologize." Jake rubbed his face. "I completely lost my head yesterday. If I could take back everything I said and start over, I would."

"I don't think anyone was thinking straight at the time." Viho shrugged. "It was a hell of a day. In fact, I'm still all fucked up. So we should probably tread carefully right now."

"Because of the baby?" His father leaned forward.

"Honestly, that's the part I'm least screwed up about." He smiled. "The idea is kind of growing on me."

"Glad to hear it." Jake seemed genuine. "Sterling deserves a good mate."

"Well, she hasn't decided yet if I fit that description." He kicked at a chunk of wood.

"She'll come around."

"Sometimes women never do." Viho trusted his gut, climbing to his feet and crossing to the shed where he kept his tools. He snagged a bottle of water and his mother's diary, which he'd wrapped in a rag.

When he returned, he found Jake staring up at him with a puzzled expression.

"It's Haiwee's journal. She quit writing in it when she left you but…there's a lot of stuff in here you'd probably like to read. Or not. Up to you."

"You're sure you don't want to keep it?" Jake cradled the package as if it were made of glass, or gold, or maybe both.

"Nah. It's not how I want to remember her." He shook his head. "There are things I read that made me lose some respect for my mom. And I think I should probably say I'm sorry too. That I took her side of things without being objective."

"You were a kid. It's not your fault. I'm proud that you were protective of her." Jake reached out as if he would take Viho's hand, but he stopped short, then awkwardly tucked his fingers in his pocket. "For the record. If I'd known about you, or even suspected, there's no way in hell I'd have gone my whole life without tracking you down. Were you happy, Viho?"

"I guess it matters more if I can be in the future, doesn't it?" He spread his legs and planted his elbows on his knees, clasping his gloved hands in front of him.

"I suppose." Jake grimaced at the obvious non-answer that was answer enough. "Just one more question about the past, if you don't mind?"

Ugh. He knew what was coming. "Go ahead."

"What about your mom? Did she have a good life?" Jake's voice cracked.

"I guess. She did the best she could. Taught me a lot. But she was lonely. Never married. Didn't have many friends on the reservation." Viho stopped short of explaining why. "She never got over you, if that's what you're asking."

"That isn't what I would have chosen for her." Jake knuckled moisture from his eye. "All this time I imagined she'd run off with another guy. Someone who could give her everything I couldn't, you know? The only thing that made it bearable sometimes was knowing she was out there somewhere, happier than I could have made her."

Crushing Jake's dreams wasn't part of Viho's plan. It figured—after years of hate and immature scheming, he found himself with the power to wound the man he'd despised, yet no will to do it. Things were no longer so black and white.

After a stretch of silence, Jake cleared his throat. "Look, I'm not trying to rush in here with fatherly advice when we don't have that kind of relationship—

or any, for that matter. But I would say that while you're on the ranch, I'd like nothing more than to get to know you. And if I could spare you—any person I know, but especially my own flesh and blood—the pain of losing someone that means as much as Haiwee meant to me, I would do it."

Viho couldn't help himself. The allure of filling the void he'd always felt so vividly was too much to resist. "So what do you think I should do?"

"Win Sterling over," Jake said in a rush, as if he'd been biting his tongue. "I've never seen her like this before. From the moment we rolled up to find you two on the side of the road, Sam and I could tell you had a connection."

"You mean you saw her shredded panties and knew we'd got it on."

"Well, I admit, there was a lot of ranting on the ride back to town." Jake laughed. "But seriously, that's not like Sterling at all. She's picky. Knows what she likes and doesn't settle. She's fierce and strong and beautiful, inside and out."

"Sounds like you love her very much." He tried not to sound bitter, but failed miserably.

"I'm not saying this to hurt you, Viho. Exactly the opposite, okay?" Jake stared straight into his eyes as he said, "Sterling Compton is more like a daughter to me than you feel like my son…for now. And if I think you're good enough for her, then I sure as hell think highly of you. Your work ethic is impressive, and the magic you've cast on these ancient gardens is miraculous. If you can make Sterling bloom like you do these plants, you're going to be a very happy man."

"I think I fucked that all up already." Viho dropped his head in his hands, never imagining he'd have a dad to discuss his love life successes…or strikeouts. It wasn't easy to admit he'd screwed up, though he was coming to understand that everyone did one time or another. It was how you recovered that counted.

"What'd you do?" It wasn't an accusation. More like curiosity. Or a willingness to talk through a solution. Weird. And awesome.

"I assumed she would marry me because of the baby."

"Ah, yeah. I'm guessing that didn't go over well."

"Nope." He flashed Jake a wry grin. "Sure didn't. But at least she didn't kick me in the nuts for jumping to conclusions."

"A distinct possibility with Sterling." Jake barked out a laugh. "So why'd you do it?"

"Huh?"

"Did you ask her because you felt obligated?"

"Hell no." Viho stood and began to pace. "I mean, after what happened…to *us*…I have some pretty strong feelings on the subject. But it's more than that. From the first minute she dared to get out of her Jeep and come up to a perfect stranger on the side of the road and offer to fix my truck…well, yeah, I just felt like…she's special. If things were different, she could be the one. And now *everything's* changed in my life."

Jake steepled his fingers. "You know, I get exactly what you're saying. I think sometimes it's like that. You recognize your soul mate right away. I did with Haiwee."

"Seriously?" Viho raised his brows.

"Yep." The word was short and simple, but Jake didn't stop there. He reached beneath the collar of his shirt for a chain around his neck and withdrew it. Threaded on it was a ring. An engagement ring. "I guess I'm nuts, but the day I met your mom I went out and bought this. I've been wearing it for damn near four decades. Never did get the chance to give it to her. The pisser of it all is that I'd planned to the night she left. I had it all laid out. Nothing spectacular or creative like the kids do these days, but I cooked a nice dinner, picked a bunch of wild flowers and had a whole speech prepared. Haiwee never showed."

"Shit." Viho plopped down beside his father again. "That sucks."

"You could say that." He reached behind his neck and unfastened the necklace. "Maybe this thing is cursed, who knows. And it's horribly old fashioned. Plain. Especially with Sterling being in the business. Well, it's probably not the right thing at all. But if there ever comes a time you want to ask her properly to marry you…"

Viho's eyes bulged as Jake held out his hand, the ring dangling from the fine gold chain.

"…I'd be honored if you'd use this."

"I don't know what to say." Viho choked on the million things swirling inside his brain simultaneously. "Th-thank you."

He accepted Jake's precious gift, staring at the glinting diamond in his palm. It wasn't plain at all. It was classic. A gorgeous solitaire, set in a delicate feminine band of yellow gold.

"It feels right, Viho. Like things that were always meant to be are starting to fall into place." Jake smiled sadly as Viho fastened the chain around his own neck and tucked the diamond inside his shirt, close to his heart. "It might take time, but I believe it's going to work out. For you and Sterling, your baby, maybe even for you and me. If that's what you want."

"I do." Viho stuck out his hand to Jake.

His father didn't accept it, though. Instead, he crossed the gap between them and gave Viho a one-armed man hug, complete with a smack on the back. "Me too, Viho. Me too."

"So then you'll help me out here?" Viho gestured to the garden.

"With these stumps? Hell no, that's a young man's job." Jake laughed.

"Not that." Viho laughed too, though he wasn't nearly as youthful as some of the hands. "What's Sterling's favorite flower? I'll need all the advantage I can get when I go see her after work."

"Ah, yes. Good plan. She likes the nontraditional stuff. More wildflower than hothouse orchid or prizewinning rose, you know? Go for peonies or gerbera daisies. Something like that."

Viho nodded, impressed with his father's insight and knowledge of plants. "I'd better get back to it if I'm going to finish up at a reasonable time to go see her. Thanks."

"You're welcome." Jake smiled. "And, son?"

"Yeah?"

"Good luck." He lifted his hand to wave goodbye.

Viho would have matched him, the gesture natural to him as well, but just then a scream from the main house split the brisk air. "Help! Someone! Viho!"

Sterling.

He dropped his axe, his gloves flying off his hands as he pumped his arms and lengthened his stride. Anything to reach her faster.

Chapter Ten

The morning after she'd confronted Viho in the barn, Sterling checked her messages, even though she knew he didn't own a phone. She ignored the concerned texts from her cousins along with the ones from her parents. There was only one person she really felt like talking to, and he wasn't interested. After last night, she wasn't sure she blamed him.

He'd only been doing what he thought was right.

And she'd pushed him away.

Shunned him without explaining that it wasn't the idea of being married to him that upset her. It was the reason that he wanted to take the plunge that set her off. More than anything, she was afraid that she'd never know if he really cared for her or if his feelings were a product of some paternal genetic coding enhanced by his history.

She debated spending the morning working on some of her projects for the shop. Her kitchen table had an assortment of wire, stones and clasps scattered across it. Or she could go into town and fill the cases they'd put into place thirty-six hours ago. When her life had been mostly normal.

Was that right?

Yesterday had been a lost cause, and the day

before it seemed like ten years ago instead.

Sterling shrugged to herself. No sense in moping around getting nothing done. She had a wicked craving for brownies. Probably more stress-related than pregnancy driven, but hey, why not use the built-in excuse while she had it?

Plus she figured dessert would make a decent peace offering.

Viho's appetite, especially his sweet tooth, was pretty legendary among the ranch hands. Sterling had overheard Clayton and Wyatt teasing him a few times when she'd still been pretending not to notice Viho not noticing her.

Ugh.

Why had they wasted weeks on foolish games?

Deciding she wasn't about to repeat her mistakes, she got to work collecting ingredients for her treats. And when they were baking, she put on a dress that would probably leave her feeling the cool fall breezes but made her look pretty dang cute, if she did say so herself.

She even took extra time with her hair and makeup, not wanting to appear frazzled or upset to anyone around the ranch who might have heard the news by now. Of course, that would be *everyone*. Most especially, she didn't want Viho to see her and think she was reeling when she actually had her eye on the future and the positive relationship they could build, regardless of what they might label it.

It might or might not be a romantic connection, but either way they were going to have to work together, not against each other, for the rest of their lives. Wouldn't it be more enjoyable to be allies rather than enemies?

And who was she fooling?

She'd wanted more of him since the taste she'd

had that day on the side of the road. The time they'd spent together in her shop had only proved she was right. There was something between them, and it could be more if they nurtured it.

Sterling packed the baked goods into a travel container, then checked her reflection in the stainless steel refrigerator door.

Viho was about to find out that no man resisted double fudge brownies baked by a Compass Girl using Vivi's secret recipe.

When Sterling rolled into the gravel lot between the main house and the barn, she saw Viho and Jake sitting on a matching set of tree stumps, clearly having a private conversation. The urge to run over there and hug them both was pretty overwhelming. So she took her goodies and slipped into the main house to check in with Vivi in the meantime.

She wondered if her grandmother would remember the total shitstorm that had erupted in the kitchen yesterday. Hopefully not.

"Vivi?" she called as she stepped through the porch door, surprised to find the lights off and no one in the living room. Usually before lunch, there would be coffee out on the counter and her grandmother would be sitting downstairs, sewing, doing crossword puzzles, reading the paper or chatting with friends and neighbors who stopped by to spend time with her while keeping a discreet eye out for the pillar of their community.

"Vivi?" Sterling called again as she poked around the screened room where her father had once had a temporary office, if ranch legends were to be believed. Still nothing.

And she hadn't been in the gardens as best Sterling could tell. Trying not to get distracted by ogling Viho, she peeked out and confirmed that the area was clear.

No Vivi.

She made a racket as she climbed the stairs to the private area of the house. Vivi couldn't hear as well as she used to, and Sterling didn't want to risk startling her. Over and over, she pled for her grandmother to answer. Still no response.

By the time she'd worked her way to Vivi's bedroom door, which was cracked open, she was terrified to go inside. What if...

There were too many terrifying scenarios to consider. Her heart pounded in her chest. A cramp in her gut had her slinging an arm around her middle as she tried one more time. "Vivi?"

A whimper mixed with a groan came in response.

Faint, but there.

Sterling flung the door open and rushed inside. The bed had been made and there was no one lying there. Sweeping the room, she ruled out all the spaces but the bathroom.

Warm incandescent light spilled from beneath the solid wood door. She knocked softly, but when no answer came, she tried the knob.

Locked.

"Seriously, Vivi. Who do you think is going to walk in on you?" Sterling spoke mostly to herself to calm her nerves. It didn't work.

She spun to the dresser and raided the mother of pearl box on top for a bobby pin. With her tool in hand, she popped the lock and held her breath. The door swung open about halfway, then stopped as it banged into something on the floor.

"Vivi!"

Sterling was even more surprised when the door flew back at her, hitting her in the side. "Oomph."

"Get the hell out!" Vivi grumbled. "I can do it myself."

"Hey, it's me. Sterling." She spoke as softly and steadily as she could manage given the trembling, which wracked her entire body. Never had her grandmother spoken to her in that tone. The doctor had warned them that aggression and anger were common in the later stages of dementia, but this was something horrifying and new for Vivi.

"I said *get out*." A bare foot kicked at the door, connecting and shoving it at Sterling again.

"Okay, I'll go, but is something wrong?" She tried to think as fast as she could. How would she get the woman out of there without making the situation worse? Sure, any number of the cowboys around could bust down the door, but how would they preserve Vivi's dignity and avoid riling her.

"I don't know." Vivi's thready reply broke Sterling's heart. "I can't remember. And I think I wet myself."

"Hey, no problem." Sterling opted to go for lighthearted and hoped the mood caught. "Who hasn't peed their pants a time or two? Remember when you took me and the rest of the Compass Girls to the county fair one year? The line for the Ferris wheel was so long that by the time we got near the front I was dancing around, looking for a bathroom. Jade told me that if I made us lose our place she would never forgive me. And, yep, I wet myself too, but I had a really pretty view while I did it. Served her right that she was in the bucket below me when I let go."

No laughter came from the other side of the door. Shit.

"Cindi, you didn't grow up in Compton Pass. I don't know who the hell you're thinking of, but it isn't me." Something crashed in the bathroom.

Sterling frantically searched for her phone but realized she'd left her purse with the brownies on the kitchen counter. Not even Vivi had a landline anymore—they'd phased it out years ago. *Shit. Shit. Shit.*

She didn't dare leave the woman alone to run for help. So she steeled her spine and wedged her foot under the door.

"Vivi, I'm coming in." Stern, she didn't give the other woman a choice. She forced the door open against a surprisingly strong resistance for an elderly lady. Afraid of hurting her or knocking her down where she could hit her head on any number of porcelain fixtures, Sterling opted for a slow, steady pressure, absorbing the kickback with her body.

Then suddenly, the force evaporated. The door winged open and she tumbled into the tiny room.

Vivi sat on the closed toilet, blinking up at her as if Sterling had been arguing with her doppelganger.

"Sterling? What's wrong? Can't a woman get some privacy around here?" Her grandmother laughed, then stood up, completely unaware of the wet spot expanding across her pants.

Only the threat of reigniting Vivi's distress kept Sterling's face from crumpling and the flood of tears searing her eyes at bay.

"Come on, Vivi." Sterling put an arm around her waist and half-carried, half-steered her toward the bedroom, desperately trying to think of some way of conning her into putting on fresh clothes without highlighting her accident. "How are you feeling today?"

"I'm fine." She smiled brightly, then glanced down, making Sterling afraid she would ask why she was wet. Instead, she said, "Why are you worried 'bout me, when *you're* the one bleeding?"

Sterling figured hallucinating was another terrible trick of her grandmother's dementia, along with rapidly vacillating moods, until she realized her thigh did feel warm and slick. In her terror, she hadn't noticed.

She looked down and saw a rivulet of blood trailing down her leg and into the carpet. As she watched, more pooled at her feet. From the impact of the door? The strain of practically carrying Vivi to bed? Or the stress of the situation?

She had no idea. But she was in over her head.

Sterling couldn't help it. She screamed, "Help! Someone!"

And then she remembered the two men she'd spotted talking in the garden a few minutes ago. "Viho!"

A whooshing sound drowned out the renewed rage-mumblings of her agitated grandmother. The room spun around her as if she were in the farmhouse from the Wizard of Oz instead of the one she'd practically grown up in. She put out a hand as she sank to the floor, but gravity didn't work as she expected, pulling her sideways.

She crashed into the runner of an antique rocking chair before landing on the ground. And though she opened her mouth to scream again, all that came out was a whimper.

Pain radiated through her and all she could think was, *No. Please. Don't be gone.*

Viho slammed through the door and tore up the stairs of the main house, following feminine shrieks. "Wake up, wake up!"

When he crashed into the bedroom, with Jake right behind him, the scene inside took a moment to sink in. He'd imagined something wrong with Mrs. Compton to cause that primal fear in Sterling's screams. Instead, it was her he saw crumpled on the floor while her distraught grandmother wailed.

The old woman yanked her own hair and tore the

buttons off her shirt.

"Holy shit," Jake gasped from behind Viho. "What the hell is going on here?"

"Jake!" Mrs. Compton yelled and moaned. The horrible sound twisted Viho's guts. "I killed her. I killed her."

"What? No!" Viho's boots unglued from the floor as he skidded the rest of the way to Sterling's side. He put his ear by her mouth and his hand on her chest, searching for signs of respiration and a heartbeat.

Thankfully, she had both.

"She's alive." Viho looked to Jake, trying to ignore the delusional woman's hysteria. His own heart had stopped, he was pretty sure.

"I'm taking Vicky downstairs. I'll send help." Jake didn't mess around. He put Mrs. Compton over his shoulder in a fireman's hold, stilled her protests with one solid arm and removed her from the room, leaving them in relative calm.

Only then did Viho gather Sterling's shoulders in the crook of his arm and tip her upward. Limp, her limbs flopped like a ragdoll's. "Sweetheart, can you hear me?"

She groaned.

"Hey. It's Viho. Looks like you took a spill." He cooed to her, trying to reach into the darkness that surrounded her. "Can you open your eyes and say hello?"

Her lashes fluttered, but she squinted against the light.

"That's good, Sterling. Real good." He rubbed her back with small circles of his fingers over her spine.

"Vivi!" she cried.

"Don't you worry. Jake's got her. She's fine. Worried about you, that's all." He might have lied, but he didn't care.

Then she shocked him by sitting up quickly, so fast that they smacked their heads together with a clunk of skull on skull.

"Ow, shit. Sterling. Lie still." He hugged her to him.

Until she moaned, "*Peanut*. I'm bleeding."

Viho's gaze winged to her legs. Her dress had hiked up when she toppled. Sure enough, blood coated her thighs. He should have spotted it sooner, but he'd been so focused on her, he hadn't even thought...

"Okay. I've got you." He scooped her into his arms and dashed from the room. "We're going to the hospital, right now. As fast as I can get us there. I'm going to do everything I can for you. And Peanut."

If she heard, she gave no indication, though tears welled in her eyes and spilled down her cheeks.

"Viho, not yet," Jake growled from the living room. "I called Sienna and Sterling's Aunt Lucy. They're nurses. They'll be here in a few."

"Plan B, Jake. She's bleeding." Viho cut himself off before he gave too many details and scared Sterling out of her mind. Because to him, it looked like a hell of a lot of blood on her alabaster skin. He clomped down the stairs, careful not to risk tripping or dropping his precious cargo. "I'm taking her to the hospital. They can meet us there."

"Keys. On the counter," Sterling relayed the pertinent info, though it seemed to cost her most of her strength.

As they passed through the living room, Viho winced. Vicky Compton thrashed in Jake's hold, scoring him with her nails, which left bright red trails on his cheek. "I told you, I don't know! I don't know what happened! What did I do? Did I kill her?"

"Don't listen, Sterling." Viho rummaged through her small purse in a hurry, though it was tough with one hand. When he located the keys to her Jeep, he tried to cover her ears by tucking her head to his chest. "She's not herself. It's not real. It's not your Vivi. Don't listen."

Traumatized—all of them, but Sterling especially—she sobbed and clung to him like a vine climbing a trellis.

Mrs. Compton's shouts trailed them out the door. "I *hate* this. Damn it. It should have been me. Let me go. Let me die!"

"No!" Sterling twisted in his grip, nearly sending them both sprawling to the gravel.

"Shh." He clamped her body close to his, still careful not to squash her, especially around her abdomen. "You can't worry about her now. Think about yourself. The baby."

Except that was exactly the wrong thing to say.

She cried harder, gasping for breath.

Viho plopped her into the Jeep and awkwardly buckled her in. Out of ideas, he jammed his hand into the front pocket of his jeans and grabbed the turquoise tortoise.

"Here." He put it in her hand and folded her fingers around the animal. "It's good luck. My mom told me so."

With that, he kissed her on the cheek, then made sure she was out of the way of the door before shutting it and crossing to the driver's side. He stuck the key in the ignition and peeled out of the driveway fast enough to sling gravel everywhere and draw curious stares from the ranch hands working near the barn.

With one hand, he jabbed the hospital into the GPS of her phone, which he'd also grabbed from her purse. Hell, he should have brought along the whole thing. Hopefully, one of the Compass Girls or Sterling's other family would bring her ID, not that anyone in town didn't already know who she was.

The glowing line drew a path through town to a facility not that far away. He decimated the speed limit as they raced toward a doctor.

When he could, he peeked over at Sterling. Her sobs had quieted to tremulous gasps, still too shallow and fast for his liking. But she seemed more alert as she stared at the stone in her palm. Her thumb rubbed the turtle's shell compulsively as if the smooth bump soothed her as it had him when he worried the same exact spot.

Distraction seemed like as good a plan as any.

"It was made by a powerful healer in our tribe," he told her.

"Beautiful," she whispered.

"I always thought so too." Viho knew his mom had been looking out for him today, when she'd practically thrown it into his hand. "And it's supposed to draw the spirit of your ancestors to you when you're in trouble. For protection. And luck."

"Did you know the hospital is named after my grandfather, JD?" she mumbled, as if she might black out again.

He couldn't have that.

"No. Tell me about him. Maybe the tortoise will find his spirit to watch over you. And Peanut."

When the Jeep rolled to a stop under the emergency room portico, Sterling held the turtle out to Viho.

"No, you keep him. Someday you'll pass him on to the baby." Viho hoped it was true. "Until then, you're in charge of it."

She bit her lip, then whispered, "What if there is no more baby?"

"We'll deal with it together."

Sterling nodded as an EMT rushed from the

automatic doors with a stretcher. They yanked open the door of the Jeep and started talking in rapid-fire. "Your cousin called. We were expecting you. Where does it hurt? How long ago did the bleeding start?"

They pulled Sterling from the car and bundled her onto the gurney, wheeling her inside before Viho could get a word in edgewise. He tried to follow, but someone stopped him. "Sir, we're going to need you to park the car out of the way so this area is clear for ambulances and other emergency vehicles."

He craned his neck to see around the orderly, but all he got a glimpse of was Sterling's bloody foot as they whisked her away.

"Then where do I go?" he asked.

"Are you family?"

"No. Yes. Well, I'm not sure. She's pregnant. I'm the father." Holy crap, it felt weird to say that out loud.

"Sorry, sir. It's best if you wait until they've examined her." The guy truly did seem apologetic, also sort of like he expected to get decked. "I've got kids of my own. I can imagine how you must feel. But you're only going to get in the way. Head up to the second-floor emergency waiting room. They'll come get you as soon as she's stable and they can tell you more about her condition."

Viho nodded as reality started to sink in. He went to shake the man's hand and realized his fingers were stained crimson. So instead he headed back to the car.

"Good luck, buddy."

"Thanks," he managed to wheeze before calmly parking, then returning to the building. It felt like the day he'd gone with his mom to get her biopsy test results. When the worst-case scenario—aggressive, inoperable cancer—became reality, his whole world had shifted.

And he felt like it could again right now.

Fucking hospitals.

Viho couldn't say how long he staggered from one end of the tiny holding pen to the other, hating the buzz of the fluorescent lighting and the smell of disinfectant. But it probably only felt like forever before Sienna, Jade and their parents flooded the area, making it seem even smaller, if possible. When Hope didn't show, he figured she was working. Probably downstairs right now.

He found himself scanning the crowd for Jake, but didn't see the guy among the gaggle of Comptons.

"Your father stayed back at the ranch. With Vicky." Cindi didn't ask first; she came right in and hugged Viho hard. "But he asked me to give you that and tell you he's praying for the best."

Sam Compton joined them, putting a strong hand on Viho's shoulder. "We are too. We all are."

Unsure of how to respond, Viho simply stood there and absorbed their affection. They seemed to understand he wasn't used to being the center of that kind of attention and gave him some space, though he wished they would have clung a little longer.

He scanned the room and the sympathetic faces ringing him. How had he inherited so many supporters in the span of a single day?

Most of all, though, he studied Sienna's expression, and then her Aunt Lucy's. The two nurses had pretty damn good poker faces, though. He couldn't tell what they were thinking or what the odds might be.

He figured they were pretty bad if neither was offering reassurances.

When the swinging door opened and a woman in a white coat emerged, it was as if everyone in the room held their breath. "Viho. I'm looking for Viho with Ms. Sterling Compton."

He stepped forward.

The doctor lowered her voice and leaned in. "She's stabilized. Her vitals are improving rapidly. Mostly I think she was dehydrated and stressed. If she keeps this up she'll be able to spend the night in her own bed, as long as you—or someone else—are there to care for her."

"I will be," he said in a rush of air.

"Your baby..." Viho's knees grew weak, anticipating the worst. "...is also doing fine."

Viho bent in half, grasping his knees to keep from toppling over.

"Viho?" Cindi Compton cried out to him as he kept them in unintentional suspense.

"She's good. They're both great." He turned to face them, not caring about the goofy grin he couldn't suppress or the dampness in his eyes. And before he could think better of it, he wrapped the staid doctor in a bear hug and swung her around while the Compass Brothers laughed and hooted.

A couple of them smacked Sam on the back.

He set the doctor down as soon as decorum sank in. "Sorry about that. Can I see her?"

The doctor grinned up at him. "Sure. As long as you don't pull that stunt with your lady."

"I promise." He chuckled, then tried to get himself together for Sterling.

"Right this way, sir." She held the door for Viho then added for the family. "Not too many visitors for her tonight. Can you limit it to just a handful, two at a time? And only for a few minutes?"

The family murmured their agreement, then began to figure out who would stay and who would go. Viho had already stopped paying attention as they wound their way through the den of rooms toward Sterling.

When the doctor ushered him in, he stutter

stepped.

Sterling looked so pale and fragile in the hospital gown. Propped up in the automatic bed, she'd placed the tortoise on her sternum. One hand rested protectively over her belly while the other stroked the figurine's shell.

When she saw him, she smiled, though it lacked its usual sparkle. "Hey."

"Hey, yourself." He crossed to her and rested half his ass on her bed while one foot stayed planted to the floor. Immediately, she leaned into him.

"Sorry for scaring you like that," she murmured.

"I was pretty sure you didn't do it on purpose." Closing his eyes, he kissed her crown.

"How is Vivi?"

"She's fine. With Jake." He hoped he wasn't exaggerating. But really, could the woman be called *fine* anymore?

"She's not. But thank you for saying that anyway." Sterling sighed. "And thank you for coming to save me today. They told me that if I hadn't gotten here as soon as I did…if my blood pressure didn't get under control…"

"It did. Don't stress yourself about what might have been." He squeezed her shoulder, figuring he could worry enough for both of them about all that stuff.

"I'm going to be more careful," she whispered. "I asked a ton of questions and got a list of books to read. Medicine and vitamins are coming too. I should have thought to do that this morning, but with how everything went yesterday…I didn't have my priorities straight."

"Sterling, neither of us has done this before." He drew away so he could look directly at her. "We're going to fuck stuff up. No matter how hard we try to do it all right. We're going to work on it together. Right?"

She nodded. "Yes."

"Good." He smiled down at her and patted the turtle on the head.

Sterling tipped her face up and reached for him, so he gave her what they both craved. A long, sweet, gentle kiss that felt like coming home.

"I'm pretty sure that's not a recommended method for keeping someone's blood pressure down," Hope Compton chided them. She jiggled a paper bag in her fist. "I brought you a whole smorgasbord of fantabulous chemicals. This should have you fixed up in no time."

Hope came closer and wiggled her way in for a hug. "You just about gave me a heart attack when I saw this order come across my desk. I'm not going to bug you for details, since I'm sure Sienna and Jade are blowing up my phone, but I had to come see you for a second."

"Thank you." Sterling blinked. "I'm so glad you came."

"And now I'm leaving, before I get in trouble from your nurses." She winked. "Take good care of her, Viho."

"Promise." He nodded and waved.

Before he could pick up where he'd left off with Sterling, a light knock came on the door. Viho grumbled and Sterling laughed. It was worth it to hear her happy.

"Hey, cuz." Jade strode into the room with Sienna on her heels. "We just passed Hope in the hall. That bitch, sneaking in here before us."

"Doing okay?" Sienna cut to the chase as she read the monitoring equipment scattered around the room. Satisfied, she nodded.

"Hell of a lot better now." She winced. "But I

think I ruined that dress you guys bought me for my birthday."

"Eh, Christmas is coming." Jade smiled. "Better rack up the presents this year, 'cause after that it'll be baby mania. Just think of all the noisy toys I can buy my mini-cuz."

"Really annoying ones," Sienna added.

"Exactly." They smiled at Sterling, then turned a little more serious, squeezing her hand in theirs.

"If we don't get out of here, your parents will probably explode," Jade said as they edged toward the door. "If you feel up to company tomorrow, call us, okay?"

"I will." Sterling smiled and wiggled her fingers.

And when they left, she turned to Viho. "Brace yourself."

"No kidding. I saw them in the waiting room, you didn't."

Her eyes grew wide. "That bad? Shit, I'm sorry."

"Sterling, you did not do anything wrong." Viho took her chin in his hand and held her gaze. "This was not your fault. Everything is okay now. Regret isn't going to help Peanut."

"You're right." She smiled up at him.

And that was how her parents found them.

"You know, Viho," Sam started as he entered the room. "I've wished a lot of things for my daughter in her life. You'll see. It's impossible not to want the best for your children. But that look in her eyes, it's one I've only seen a few times. And I'm so happy that she has you to put it there."

Viho swallowed hard as Sterling patted his cheek.

Her mom spoke more quietly, but what she said rocked him harder. "Even more, I knew my daughter had more love to give than most. And I'm so glad that she's found a man like you who will appreciate that gift and never take it for granted."

Instead of responding to the Comptons, he looked at Sterling and promised, "I won't."

"I know," she whispered.

"Do you want us to wait and take you home?" Her father might have approved, but he was still her dad. And he gave her an out to any potentially sticky situations.

Sterling looked from her parents to Viho. "If you don't mind driving me, I'd rather go with you."

"Of course." He held her fingers with one hand, squeezing them lightly.

Her mom and dad took turns kissing her and saying goodbye. Hand in hand, they made their way to the door. At the last minute, Cindi turned and leveled one of her megawatt smiles at Sterling and Viho. "And I'm so sorry, I don't think I've said congratulations. To you both. I'm *thrilled* that we're going to be grandparents."

"Thank you," Viho and Sterling said in unison.

They looked at each other and smiled, still holding hands, just like Sterling's mom and dad.

Viho couldn't stop himself. He reached up and rubbed the center of his chest. Sterling seemed to notice him touching the small bulge beneath his shirt, but before she could ask him what caused it, the nurse returned with discharge paperwork. Eager to be home, in her nice comfortable bed—hopefully allowing Viho to hold her through the night—she forgot about her curiosity.

Together they listened to a long lecture about what she should and shouldn't be doing, the dosage and schedules for taking the various vitamins and medicines she'd been prescribed, and scheduled the first of what seemed to be many regular doctor visits.

By the time Viho carried Sterling to the Jeep and

buckled her in, she was done in.

"Sleep, Sterling." He cupped her cheek in his hand and kissed the tip of her nose. "I've got you. We can talk tomorrow, okay?"

Her response garbled as she drifted off, safely in his care.

Chapter Eleven

Sterling blinked as she floated from deep sleep into consciousness. The first thing she was aware of was having to pee. The second—a much nicer revelation—was that a full-length combination pillow and radiator transformed her comfy bed into the ultimate sleeping palace.

"Viho."

"Good morning," he rumbled with the sexiest not-quite awake voice she'd ever heard. Had he slept as well as she had?

Thank goodness it was Sunday and he had the day off. Not that her family would hold him to his schedule considering the drama of the day before. Still, she knew that if it had been any other day, he'd have dragged his ass out of their cozy haven and gone to work, making the most of each minute that ticked by in the dying year.

When he committed to something, he did it right.

"Hey." She smiled up at him, then allowed her eyes to flutter closed once more as he swept her hair from her face with long, gentle passes of his broad palm. The tips of his fingers traced the arch of her brows, smoothing them into place too. If he kept going, she was pretty sure he could put her entire world in order.

"How are you feeling?" He dropped butterfly kisses on her forehead then cheeks, waking more than her mind in the process.

She stretched, testing the soreness of her muscles, happy to report none. The medicine they'd given her to combat early pregnancy discomfort seemed to have kicked in too. For the first time in weeks, she felt fabulous. What had women done before these groundbreaking drugs had been invented? "Terrific."

How could she be anything else when she had Viho by her side and their baby growing safely inside her? It hadn't taken more than an instant yesterday, when she'd feared losing one or both, to understand what she craved, even if it scared her too.

Sterling rolled fully onto Viho, nuzzling his neck and breathing deep of his rich, earthen scent. It made her calm, yet excited. Soothed and inflamed all at once.

"I like waking up with you in my bed." She nibbled her way across his jaw to his lips. Her thumbs brushed his collarbones while her fingers curled around his powerful shoulders, kneading what she could reach.

"You don't hear me complaining about it, do you?" He glided his hands along her ribs to land on the upper swells of her ass, covered by a long sleep-shirt. "You snore a little less loudly than the guys in the bunkhouse too. Bonus."

She laughed as she lifted up to tweak one of his nipples. "Hey, I do *not* snore."

"Honestly, I wouldn't know. I haven't slept that hard in years." Viho squeezed her bottom as he craned his neck for a kiss.

She obliged him, tipping her head forward so that their lips could meet. Gently and slowly. They teased each other with tender licks and the prodding of tongues. Sterling could have made out with him all day.

Except after a minute or five, it wasn't enough. She wanted to be connected to him.

After everything that had happened, it felt like they needed to rejoin each other. Make up. The old fashioned way. Sterling inched her nightgown up until it wadded around her waist, revealing her lacy panties. She got to her knees with her thighs splayed on either side of Viho's. The new angle pressed her against him deliciously.

"Are you sure you're up for this?" His eyes pinched at the corners.

"Yep. And I don't have to ask if you are." A wiggle of her hips confirmed it. He was tempting her with the thick bulge in his briefs.

"A boner won't kill me, Sterling." He shifted, as if that would make his arousal less obvious.

"The doctor cleared me for loads of steamy—but gentle—sex." She grinned. "No joke, I asked. Didn't want to deprive either of us if I didn't have to. I mean, if that's what you want. I was hoping, after yesterday, we might be back on that track."

"Seriously?" Viho stripped her shirt over her head, threw it to the floor, then wrapped his fingers around the back of her neck. A sound suspiciously like the purr of a jungle cat came from his throat when their bare chests pressed together. He held her as he kissed her, more deeply and fully than he ever had before.

"Yeah." A breathless rasp would have to suffice as a response. "Except…"

"What's wrong?"

"Nothing major. I just have to use the restroom." She ducked her head, embarrassed. "I've never lived with a guy before. This is going to take some getting used to."

Viho froze. "Is that what's happening here? Am I moving in?"

"You don't want to?" Sterling sat up, slipping off of him. With her knees tucked under her, she hugged a pillow to her like a shield.

"I didn't say that." He propped himself on his side, supported by a bent elbow and with his head in one hand. "I'm afraid to make any moves here, Sterling. To assume anything. I don't want to scare you away or take more than you're offering. But if you're asking me to shack up with you…"

"I am." She worried her lower lip between her teeth.

"Then yes, I'd love to." A smile crossed his face. "You've got to be tidier than my current roommates. Do you think your dad and uncles…or, hell, *my* dad…are gonna come through here with pitchforks and rifles when they find out? Mind you, that won't make me change my mind. I just want to brace myself, you know?"

"I'm pretty sure they're aware of how babies are made." Sterling shrugged. "What's the harm in it now? I think they'll respect us more for working on our relationship than if we had a one-night stand and washed our hands of each other. Besides, it's empty here lately with the rest of the Compass Girls off doing their own thing. They won't like me being alone, in case something happens… I could take care of myself, but they are a teensy bit overprotective. If you haven't noticed."

Viho laughed. "Yeah, I think I got that impression."

"Anyway, maybe there's a perk to being the last Compass Girl to find her guy. I've inherited the house by default." She shrugged. "It's a nice starter home for our family, right?"

"It's perfect." Viho took her fingers, kissing her knuckles. "I've never had a place of my own before.

Not that I consider your house mine or anything."

"You should." She smiled. "Ours."

"If that's so, then you'd better go take care of business so we can celebrate properly." He waited until she'd slipped from the bed, then snaked his palm around her thigh, halting her. "Thank you, Sterling. For being so adaptable and generous. You have no idea how much you've given me already. More than I dared to dream of."

She couldn't find her voice, so she nodded instead, blinking back tears.

Refusing to cry on such a glorious morning, she rushed into the bathroom.

A few minutes later, Sterling poked her head out of the bathroom door. "I think I'd better grab a quick shower before we get to the good stuff. I can feel the hospital grime on me still."

"Hang on." Viho rose from the bed, flashing acres of dark skin and flexing muscles beneath. "I have a better idea."

It felt a little strange, more intimate than fucking on the side of the road, to allow him into her personal space. But still, she stepped aside and made room for him to join her. When he spotted the garden soaking tub that had been one of her only insistences in the building of the house, he perked up.

"Room enough for us both. Excellent." He flipped on the water, testing the temperature with his finger. When satisfied, he asked, "Do you have any bubble bath?"

She shook her head no.

"Epsom salts?"

"Ah, yeah, actually. I think Sienna kept some around for when the hands asked her to treat random bumps and bruises."

"Great. Hop in here." He held her elbow as if she

might slip and fall when she'd soaked in this tub a million times before. "I'll be right back."

"Where are you going?"

"Nowhere far." He grinned as he headed out.

She guessed that was the truth, since he didn't even have pants on.

In under a minute he returned with a handful of purple blossoms. "Hope you don't mind. I noticed this hybrid lavender out front. It seemed to be growing mostly wild."

"I didn't even know that's what it was." Sterling shrugged. "It's pretty and it smells nice—that's about the extent of my knowledge."

"It's also good for relieving stress, making your skin soft, increasing circulation and a bunch of other stuff." He wrung the plant in his hands, then sprinkled the blossoms into the water. Some floated and some swirled in the current. The scent grew stronger too.

"You could be on to something there, Viho." She sighed then patted the space she'd left behind her. "But I think I'd feel even better if you were in here with me."

"That I can do." He dropped his underwear, allowing her to stare at him nude for a bit. Then he stepped into the tub and slid his legs on either side of her. Even in the oversized soaker, he had to bend his legs to fit comfortably.

Sterling rested her arms on his legs and snuggled into his chest. Breathing deeply, she filled her lungs with lavender steam.

Viho used her loofa and began to wash her. She felt like a pampered member of a harem where he was the sultan. It was a nice feeling to be taken care of so well. To surrender control and enjoy the treatment.

"A girl could get used to this." She hummed when he paid special attention to her breasts. They must have been extra dirty.

When she grew restless, he moved on and circled her belly.

Was he imagining the changes that were coming? She was.

And for a second, her bliss slipped away as if it were swirling the drain between her feet.

"Viho?"

"Yeah?"

"Would you be here with me now, like this, if I hadn't gotten pregnant?"

"I know you're afraid this is about the baby, but it's not, Sterling." He held her against his chest, creating a waterfall of silky lavender water by cupping his hand and spilling it over her repeatedly. "I would feel this way about you even if we'd hadn't gotten lucky by some fluke of nature. Hell, I spent weeks trying to resist you. I've seen you care for Mrs. Compton. Heard the Compass Boys brag endlessly about how cool you are. I admire your drive in your business and the connection you have with nature's beauty. How you bravely go for what you desire when you see it. I care about you because you're the woman you are, not because of the child you're carrying. That's just icing."

Sterling didn't realize how strongly she'd harbored that doubt inside her.

Until his sweet reassurance unknotted her worries.

Tears splashed into the tub as they fell from her face. "Thank you, Viho."

"I didn't do anything. You're amazing all on your own."

Utterly relaxed, Sterling let herself veg in his care. She hadn't realized the water had cooled until Viho drew a line with his finger down the goose bumps on her arm.

"Time to get out." He sounded as reluctant to leave as she was. Still, he shifted, lifting her from the tub and standing her up on the mat long enough to dry her with a fluffy towel. Then he did the same, much more hastily, for himself before carrying her into the bedroom.

He set her on the bed, then nudged her hip.

"Roll over."

Wondering what he had in mind, she complied, hoping it was something kinky.

Except it was even better.

Viho climbed on top of her, straddling her ass. He snagged a tube of lotion off her nightstand, then warmed it between his palms before slathering her back with the fruity-scented cream. Rubbing it in bit by bit, he proceeded to give her a massage that beat the one she'd had at Compton Pass's new spa for her birthday treat from the Compass Girls, who'd really just wanted an excuse for a girls' day out.

Sterling moaned when his thumbs pressed along either side of her spine, loosening the last of the lingering tension that hadn't been obliterated by his lavender infusion. He worked every muscle within reach, including some she hadn't realized were so taut.

When the heels of his hands released knots in her ass and upper thighs, she sighed. Her legs splayed open as she went completely floppy.

Viho whispered praise as he diverted for a moment and rubbed the valley between her thighs, brushing her pussy with his knuckles. But then he was gone, sitting on his heels at her feet as he rubbed the arches and even each toe in turn.

But it wasn't until he'd worked his way from her shoulders down her arms to her hands, that she realized exactly how erogenous the palm and fingers could be.

If he didn't move on to making love to her soon,

she would die. She was sure of it.

So when he told her to flip over and seemed like he would start all over again, she took matters into her own hands.

Sterling grabbed his forearm and tugged, toppling him beside her on the bed.

He chuckled and scooped her up to avoid squashing her with his gargantuan frame.

Spooning her, he naturally fit against her in all the most sensational places. His hard-on sprang between her legs, where he allowed his cock to nestle into the valley of her pussy, thrilling them both with the almost-penetration of his thick erection.

On fire, Sterling flexed all her muscles, then released them, rocking a bit against him.

And when he dipped the slightest bit inside, they both moaned. He held her tight, pinning her torso to his with one forearm locked above her breasts. His other hand was free to roam her body, toying with her breasts then traveling along until he could strum her clit in time to the advancement of his cock within her with each successive arch of her body.

He proved over and over that he had far more control than she did.

And he wasn't afraid to employ it to enhance her arousal.

"Please, Viho. I can't wait any more. I want you inside me. All the way. Please."

"I can't resist you begging like that." He angled her head toward him so he could kiss her as he slid inside her fully, binding them.

Sterling moaned her appreciation into his mouth, and he swallowed her cry of desire.

Only then did he begin to thrust inside her. Maddeningly slowly, fucking her with strokes that took his blunt head all the way to the ring of muscles guarding her opening before he sank inside her balls deep once more.

Over and over again.

Sterling shivered as passion rolled from her fingers through her whole body and out her toes. Nothing in her sexual experience could compare to making love with Viho. And she knew that was what it was. This wasn't fucking. Or sex for the sake of a quick, hard orgasm. It was something more meaningful. Deeper and more powerful.

A bond they were forming. One that could be strong enough to last for life.

When his hand shifted upward, coming to cradle her throat, she couldn't help herself.

Without warning, Sterling's whole body quaked. She came around Viho's cock, squeezing him and attempting to wring him dry. But he lunged into her, embedding himself fully, and rode out her orgasm with only his fingers tapping her clit to keep time with his heavy breathing in her ear.

"Viho," she panted. "That was—"

"Beautiful," he finished for her. "I can't wait to see you do it again. And again."

"I can't." She shook her head, dragging her damp hair against his chest.

"You will."

He rolled forward, pressing her into the mattress, still careful to keep his full weight off her. Face down, she allowed herself to go completely limp as her body still quivered. The braid of Viho's hair slipped off his shoulder and landed on hers, the slight sting making her jump.

And moan.

Viho nuzzled her ear, nipping the lobe, then promised, "Someday we're going to explore your submissive side more. Not now, not like this. But we will."

Her sigh was cut off by a moan when he began to move inside her again, rejuvenating the smoldering arousal in her nerve endings. He pumped into her with infuriating carefulness. So she helped him out by rocking backward to meet his thrusts.

She got away with one or two twitches of her ass, enhancing the motion of his fucking, before he pinned her tighter. Only for a few strokes, an unmistakable reminder.

And when he released her, she tried to play by the rules.

But after a few more unbearably deep drives, she found herself unconsciously participating, undulating her hips in counterpoint to his shuttling.

"Sterling, if you can't be still and calm, I'll tie you up. I swear I will," he growled in her ear as he tapped her ass. And she thought she might come again on the spot.

She whimpered and writhed harder beneath his restraining weight. With her head turned to the side, she could peer up at him as he studied her reactions up close and personal.

"You like the idea?" Viho gave her that special wolfish smile she loved so much. It might have made some people nervous. Not her.

"Mmm. Yes." She admitted it.

"Then tell me," he murmured against her cheek, hardly allowing her room to breathe. "Do you have any scarves in your closet?"

"Yes. They're hanging from the hook behind the door." She didn't hesitate for a second.

Neither did Viho.

He climbed off her, making her moan at the loss of his cock.

"Don't worry, I'm coming right back. Promise."

Crossing the room with two enormous strides, he whipped open the door and collected what he'd gone for, returning with a fistful of hand-dyed silk.

"This will do." He hummed as she rolled onto her back and spread-eagled herself without waiting to be told.

"I couldn't have imagined a woman like you, Sterling." Viho spoke to her as he bound first one wrist, then the other. He tied them to the headboard before moving on to her feet. The wide band of silk hugged her ankle, the material cool then warming quickly against her heated skin. "Someone made for me. Someone I could give all of myself to without hiding anything. You understand me. Shadows and light."

"Because I'm the same." She owed it to him to be honest.

"You are. And I can hardly believe you're real." He secured her other leg, then traced one finger down the arch of her foot. When she jerked, she unwittingly tested his knot work, finding it thorough, like everything else he did.

A gasp left her throat as he leapt onto the bed between her spread legs. She couldn't close them. Didn't want to. Though she expected him to climb up her body and plunge inside her, he didn't. He continued to ratchet her desire higher by licking her anklebone, then kissing up her calf as he kneaded her shins in a pale imitation of his earlier massage.

These touches were less concentrated on healing and more intent to inflame her.

It worked.

She squirmed, trying to rush him to no avail.

But he made it worth the wait as he caressed, sucked, nipped and generally worshipped every inch of her on his path upward. Though when he reached the crease of her thigh, he teased, skirting the moist folds of her pussy and lavishing his attention on her belly instead.

Of course, while he made love to her, tenderly, with his mouth, his hands wandered to her breasts and lightly, so very gently, toyed with her nipples. She appreciated his finesse since they'd become sensitive, almost to the point of pain.

Somehow his touches made the ache subside, or morph into something she could definitely enjoy. And just when she thought he couldn't be more skilled, he lowered his mouth and applied his tongue to her clit.

Sterling would have rocketed off the bed if she hadn't been tied. She jerked against the bonds, only making herself hornier when she realized that she was his captive. The bastard chuckled against her pussy, thoroughly enjoying her display of both wanton desire and helplessness.

It didn't matter that she'd lost control of the situation when he read her signals so adeptly.

Viho lapped at her slit, drawing the arousal from her while humming his appreciation. The resulting sound waves amplified his influence on her, incinerating the last of her inhibitions.

"Please, Viho. Make me come." She moaned, unsure of whether her reaction had grown so intense because of him or because of the changes her pregnancy was beginning to wreak on her body. Somehow, though, she suspected it had more to do with the man than her hormones.

He didn't obey immediately.

Instead, he fed the tip of one finger into her pussy, barely poking the fat digit inside her before withdrawing. He stretched her slowly, bit by bit, more patiently than she could ever have managed if his cock were within her grasp again.

She supposed that was the point of his little

display.

And when he fully embedded a single finger and began working on a second, she quaked, already hovering on the edge of another orgasm. His probing deepened and expanded as he scissored the fingers inside her. He massaged her internally as well as he'd done to her exterior—or better.

When he pressed, with deliberate pulses, on the spot just above her pubic bone, Sterling could no longer resist the call of her body. He tended her as if she were one of his plants, pruning her responses, shaping her experience until she blossomed under his ministrations.

Sterling called his name as she crested, but he was well aware of her body's capitulation to his sensual demands. He wrung every bit of rapture from her before ascending, giving her a taste of her own ecstasy from his full, talented lips.

And when she thought she couldn't get any more satisfied, he slipped his cock inside her.

Viho began to drive into her with shallow, persistent jabs that were no substitute for animalistic humping. Or so she thought, until he adjusted the angle of his penetration and zeroed in on a wonderful place within her.

Her eyes went wide, and he laughed even as he fucked.

Enjoyment radiated from him. Not just the sensual kind either. He smiled down at her, relishing their time together as much as the pleasure they concocted.

He was so gloriously male, and entirely focused on her, that she thought she might melt.

When he entwined his fingers with hers, enhancing the sensation of being captured, she wished she could wrap her legs around his waist and hug him tight to her. She didn't have to worry, though—he wasn't about to abandon his post.

It was the kind of sex where the journey was more important than the destination. The kind she'd read about but never had before. She forgot about coming and instead gloried in the moment. The connection. The pure intimacy of sharing the experience with Viho.

He took her to a place far beyond those she'd ever gone before.

And if the intensity of his gaze or the sweetness of his kisses were any indication, the same was true for him.

Neither of them spoke, choosing to communicate exclusively with their bodies.

His hips never stopped their incessant rocking, like a pendulum on the world's sexiest clock. He fucked her with the precision of a metronome, pushing and pulling in time to his own unrelenting beat.

Until she'd had enough of his reserve. "Viho, that feels so good."

"Uh." He grunted his agreement.

"I love the way your cock stuffs me. How you stretch me around you and make me feel so full of you." She flashed him a wicked grin when, finally, his stride hiccupped.

"Not fair, Sterling." He imparted even more sensation as he rode her slightly harder and a bit erratically.

"Why not?" She nipped his lip when he came close enough.

"I want to wait for you," he groaned.

"You have more stamina than all the other guys I've been with." Reassuring him felt right, and it wasn't a lie. He was a machine in bed. "You've given me so much. Take, Viho. I'm here for that too. To give you what you need."

He groaned as he plunged into her fully, then retreated almost to the point of dislodging himself.

"It's okay, Viho. I want you to let go. Find your pleasure in me. Fill me. Flood me. Come on." She urged him as his ironclad control frayed around the edges.

"Yes!" he shouted as his head fell back for a moment. He fucked deep and thoroughly a few more times before going still above her. "Yes. Sterling!"

He soaked her with his come, saturating her with his pleasure. She swore she could feel the ethereal joy as clearly as the scalding fluid that painted her pussy with his seed. Good thing he couldn't get her pregnant again. It was no wonder the Vasalgel had been no match for his impressive release.

The man was practically a sex god.

And he proved it.

"Do you think you're so clever?" he said between kisses on her nose, mouth and over her eyes. His cock softened within her, but that didn't stop him from pumping a little, making her rethink her strategy as her body still pulsed with warmth and some excitement.

Contentment too, and that would be plenty.

"Kind of." She grinned up at him.

"Well, shows what you know. Now I can concentrate on driving you crazy again." He bit her neck softly, making her eyes fly open at the resulting electric jolt straight down her spine.

"What?" She tugged at her restraints. "Viho, I'm good. Seriously."

"Think you've had enough, do you?" He lifted a brow.

"I'm never going to be horny again." Sterling admitted.

He took that as a challenge. "I'll be the judge of that."

His cock slipped from her along with a trickle of moisture. Instead of pausing to clean her off with a more traditional method, Viho surveyed her pussy, messy from his release. He flicked a glance at her as he descended.

"I like seeing my claim on you." He shrugged. "I know I'm probably not supposed to admit that, but…it's true."

Sterling didn't think she was woman enough to confess that she liked his possessive streak, just a bit. So instead, she drummed her heels, as much as she was able, in response to the first contact of his mouth on her iced folds.

At one with everything natural, she shouldn't have been surprised by his acceptance of their mingled fluids as just another normal part of them. He devoured her, proving over and over, that he would always have the upper hand when it came to delighting his partner.

No matter what, he would satisfy her.

Beyond even what she realized she needed.

Viho dipped his fingers inside her, withdrawing them to study the mark he'd left within her. He played with the result of their passion, toying with the cream inside her to allow him to slip and slide against her sensitive flesh.

The idea alone had her gritting her teeth to keep from coming so soon.

He chuckled against her, only making her dilemma worse.

Until he paused long enough to say, "That's what I thought."

Before she could gather her wits enough to make some retort, he'd surrounded her clit with his lips and began to suckle with a light and rapid pulsing pressure that she had absolutely no chance at resisting.

"Viho!" she screamed as she shattered, this time

losing all of herself in the process. She unraveled so thoroughly, she wasn't sure she would ever be able to be put back together. Or not in the same way she had existed before.

Still he didn't abandon her. No, he brought her down slowly, feeding her his finger and tongue until the spasms faded to aftershocks and then those diminished, leaving a gentle glow in their wake. Only then did he kiss her belly before untying her limbs and blanketing her with his body.

As Sterling lounged beneath him, steeped in passion and bliss, she realized that Viho had won more of her than a partner in raising a child. He'd stolen part of her heart. And she didn't ever want it returned.

It might take a while for it to grow from this spark to something that burned as fierce and bright as the love of her mother and father or the other Compass Brothers and their wives, but it existed. And if they nurtured it, it would thrive.

Feeding the fire could make it burn forever, granting them a lifetime of warmth and light.

She chided herself for getting so sappy after a handful of spectacular orgasms, until he spoke and sealed the deal.

"Would you mind if I raided your kitchen to make us breakfast in bed?" he asked. "I'll even bring some of those brownies I found out on the counter last night. They were fucking great."

Oh yeah, he was *definitely* a keeper.

Chapter Twelve

Jake sat with Vicky on the porch of the main house a couple of months after the incident with Sterling. For him, he'd considered that the beginning of the true end. Though she'd declined by degrees, Vicky had never fully recovered to even her previous level of alertness.

Sam and the rest of the Compass Brothers had agreed that for the foreseeable future he should spend his days tending to her, since they needed to be sure that whoever kept her company could take charge physically if necessary. They wouldn't risk one of the women after what had nearly happened that day.

He shuddered.

Tucking the quilt tighter around Vicky, he stood and stoked the blaze in the fire pit, which allowed them to get some fresh air despite the steady slide into winter that had already begun. Most times they sat here, saying nothing, Vicky lost in her own world while the sounds, smells and sights of the ranch formed a backdrop for her memories.

It seemed fitting that he was here with her, near the end.

They'd always shared a bond. The understanding of the pain of a lost mate. Vicky had been there for him, a mother, mentor and friend. And now he would be there for her. Until she no longer required his assistance.

He'd gotten so used to his quiet guard that it shocked him when Vicky spoke. Lucidly.

"Jake?"

"Hey there, pretty lady." Surprised, and thrilled, he rushed to her side and knelt so they were at eye level. "How are you today?"

"There's no good answer to that, is there?" She shrugged. "Let's not pretend, Jake. Things are as they are."

He could have plopped onto his ass, she sounded so much like her old self. Spunky and direct. Sure of herself. How he'd missed her!

Vicky stared down at him. "Winter is coming."

"Are you cold? I can take you inside." He shrugged out of his coat and layered that on top of her blankets.

"No, I'm ready for it, Jake." She smiled. "Sometimes those snowy days are best, when you forget about going outside and stay in your cozy house, surrounded by loved ones."

He remembered a lot of such days. When they'd done the bare minimum, feeding and watering the animals then racing inside to enjoy Vicky's spiced hot apple cider. Card games, trash talk and home cooked meals. They *were* good times.

"And somehow, when it's coldest, a new year begins. A place for spring to jump out from. Like most things in life, it's a matter of perspective," she continued. And it'd been so long since she'd spoken like this, making sense, that he didn't dare interrupt.

"I've seen a lot of years, Jake. A lot of winters. Some of them colder and longer than others. But there's always the chance to start again. I want you to remember that." She lasered her blue gaze at him. "I don't worry about my children. They're living their own lives as they should. But you...I've always been troubled about you, my friend."

"I'm good, Vicky." He shrugged. "Don't waste time thinking about that."

"You will be." She nodded. "If you embrace the new year, I understand that some things cannot be replaced. But you have a chance now. To know your son. Your grandbaby. To fill the winter inside you with light and warmth. It won't be the same as a sunny summer day. But it will save you from freezing to death."

He was stunned that she remembered Sterling was pregnant. Almost so much that he took longer than usual to process the rest of what she said. But when he did, the words hit him like an angry bull. Goring him.

There was a time when he'd used sex to thaw that part of him. But he'd outgrown that phase of his life. Mostly. What she said made sense. And already he knew that spending time with Viho these past eight weeks had begun to chip away at the layers of ice that had preserved him when he couldn't handle a world without Haiwee.

Other things had helped. Sterling, her brother, their cousins.

Being lucky enough to do what he loved every day of his life.

But Vicky was right—there were times when he'd imagined himself frozen to the core. A lost cause. A man without a purpose.

"If you repeat this to my children, or theirs, frankly I'll pretend like I'm demented and you heard what you wanted in my rambling. I've got a little practice." She shrugged and flashed him a devious grin.

Oh, this could *not* be good.

Jake nodded solemnly.

"I'm telling you this because I know you understand. There are times when I have prayed to forget. Permanently." She wrung her hands. "What would it be like, if I hadn't spent all these years with the constant knowledge that my soul mate was gone?"

A white-hot poker stabbed Jake in the chest. He knew that pain, lived with the regret every day. That he hadn't looked harder. In his heart, he could have guessed where Haiwee had fled to, but he'd let his own doubts encourage him to stay still.

He'd convinced himself that she left because he wasn't good enough. Couldn't provide for her in the way she was used to as the daughter of a powerful family. He was no Compass Brother, only a ranch hand. And now he'd never see her again. He'd live with that bitterness until he died, knowing he could have done more.

And hadn't.

"If I could simply forget he was gone, I could be happy again, Jake." She turned to him with tears in her eyes. "My final days would be spent at peace. The kind I haven't known in over twenty years. I know that it is selfish. But I have held off the winter for over two decades. Is it wrong to want that pain to ease?"

"No, Vicky. It's not." Jake felt the ragged wound in his own heart. He knew as long as he was alive, it would never fully heal. Scab over, maybe. But it would scar.

Had already.

"I feel most days like I'm living in a fog," Vicky continued. "It's not so bad, that aimless floating. But when I surface. And I remember." She gasped. "It hurts, Jake."

"Where?" He was afraid she was having a stroke or something else he couldn't combat.

"Here." She tapped her chest, over her heart. "Worse, every time. It's a cruel punishment. And I'm ready to stop living in pain."

The piercing look she gave him chilled him to the core. No amount of wood on the fire would melt that terror. "Uh, Vicky. You're not asking me to—"

"No. No need to smother me with a pillow." She chuckled, then patted his hand. "Nothing like that. It's just that none of us knows what waits for us beyond this life. I think I'd like to spend what time I have left with those who have gone before me. Is that terrible to admit?"

Jake thought of JD. Plus Snake and all the other old-timers who'd passed on. A whole generation of ranchers lost. And he knew there were more, from before he'd found Compass Ranch and the community it had founded. He wished he could visit them himself. Maybe Vicky's illness wasn't exactly the curse it seemed.

"No, Vicky. That sounds…kind of nice."

She nodded. "I think so too, dear."

For a while longer they sat in companionable silence.

"So you'll explain, to my family? Where I've gone? It's a lovely place." She looked up to him. "I have lived a fantastic life. One any woman could hope for, and I am happy to relive the best moments of it. The barn dances…our children being born…their children…but mostly, my husband…JD…"

And when she trailed off, the glassy look he'd gotten so familiar with lately hazing her once-clear eyes again—more completely—he knew she had gone. For good.

"Goodbye, Vicky." A lone tear trailed down his cheek. "Say hello to JD for me, would you?"

Chapter Thirteen

"I'm nervous." Sterling chewed the nail on her index finger as she milled about the lobby of Compton Pass's tattoo shop.

"Because of the baby?" Hope asked. "We checked with your doctor. You're all clear."

"It's not that," she answered. Once Viho saw what she intended, he'd know how she felt. It would be impossible to ignore a declaration like that. Was she ready?

"Then why? It's not like it's permanent or something," Jade ribbed her. "Oh, wait. It is."

"Come on, chicken." Sienna smiled. "If I can do it, you can too."

"I've always had a thing for women with ink." Viho bent down and kissed her, sexy and sweet. The past two months had flown by and she could no longer imagine a world in which he wasn't by her side each time she needed him or as they enjoyed the simple moments in life together. Things in the old Compass Girl cabin were comfortable. Someone to come home to, to share the evenings with and make love to every night before bed.

Her life was so much more than she could have dreamed of before fall set in. It would always be her favorite time of year from now on because the colors of the leaves, the scent of pumpkins and spice, all of it reminded her of falling in love, softly and gradually, with him.

Still, she couldn't deny that it had happened.

She smiled into his eyes as they parted their lips. She was ready.

"Well, that settles it, then." Sterling couldn't resist zooming up for a final taste before one of the artists cleared her throat and invited the four Compass Girls to take their places in the shop where they'd simultaneously get matching designs in honor of their family. *Vivi.*

"Imagine our dads doing this the hard way? With that old dude, Snake, and his ancient equipment? At least modern methods aren't painful," Hope speculated.

"We'll see what you think of that when you're finished." Wyatt patted his woman on the shoulder. "You're pretty brave. I've seen grown men afraid of all those needles. Especially since you're going big your first time out."

"Hey, Jade, were you lying to me? Does it hurt? They still use needles? Not some fancy laser thingy?" Hope's smile faded as her suspicions grew.

The other three Compass Girls snorted and giggled. Even the guys they'd brought along had a hard time containing their amusement. Of course it wasn't pain-free. Nothing that mattered in life was.

"You bitches!" Hope shrieked as the first dots buzzed into her skin.

Sterling tried not to laugh too hard since she didn't want the lines of her design to be fuzzy. That would be fitting punishment for their prank, though. The Compass Ranch logo would look pretty fine on her forearm, surrounded by a riot of flower blossoms from Vivi's garden. Each one represented a person in her family, who had chosen their favorite and added it to their bouquet.

The four women had arranged the flowers in their matching designs very precisely by the season in which they bloomed. They even included some evergreen branches and a poinsettia to celebrate how Comptons could flourish in the harshest conditions.

For several hours—maybe even three or four, she kind of lost track—they were mostly quiet. Somber and introspective as the matching portions of their designs took shape.

Sterling admitted the fall foliage plus the orange and deep purple of the mums that represented her were her favorite. Like their fathers before them, each of the women had chosen one section to personalize. And she knew exactly what she wanted in that precious spot on her skin.

Forever.

Indelibly etched.

And hopefully the man beside her would understand the significance.

She took a deep breath and figured this endurance test of her pain threshold would be good practice for labor. A while passed before the artist broke her from her wandering thoughts.

"Okay, have you decided what we're doing here?" She tapped the blank spot at the center of the identical design with her gloved finger some time later. They'd all agreed to have their artists freehand their individual components, both to keep them a surprise and to fit the flow of their bodies once the rest of the art had been established.

"Yes." Sterling stared at Viho, who'd sat beside her the entire session, holding her hand and murmuring his approval. "I want a set of shears. Because every garden needs someone to tend it. I also want a dove, flying above it all, keeping an eye on things."

Viho cleared his throat, and she knew he was thinking of Haiwee, finally free of all the weighty things in life that had kept her grounded. She reached out to solidify their connection even as the proof of it became part of her forever. With his other hand, he cupped her baby bump.

She beamed up at him while still speaking to the artist. "And right on that rock there, can you add a little turtle?"

"Sure thing. It'll fit great. Kind of looks like it needed something else right there." The artist got to work making it a reality.

"Sterling, I know this is probably a weird time to have this conversation, but I figure you can't run away from me at the moment." Viho spoke softly, but it wasn't exactly a large space. All three of the other Compass Girls stared over at them, not even pretending to give them some privacy.

For that matter, Liam, Wyatt, Clay and Daniel seemed pretty damn interested in their business all of a sudden too.

"Uh, okay." She winced as she realized how unsure she sounded. It wasn't often he got this serious, and the times that he had, she hadn't always responded well. She hoped he realized she wasn't so afraid anymore. That he had won her over.

It was just that they didn't have the best track record when it came to deep conversations about their future. Though she would really like to change that.

"So here goes." He cleared his throat. "I love you, Sterling Compton. I think I have since the moment I met you."

"And knocked you up." Jade added her editorial commentary.

"Shhh…" Hope shot their cousin a death-ray

glare.

Sterling would have squirmed if she wasn't cognizant of the artist trying her best to pretend like this wasn't happening in her chair. With no escape, she wasn't prepared for what she thought he was about to say. To ask.

And she couldn't bear to turn him down either.

"I love you too, Viho." She squeezed his fingers.

"And because I think I know you better now, I just wanted to tell you that I'm not going to ask you to marry me. Not today. And not ever."

"What the—?" Sienna sat up since everyone had abandoned the pretense of tattooing at that news flash. Actually, Sterling realized they were finished when the artists began to wipe the blood from their shiny new art.

Sterling smiled wider. No pressure.

"In fact," he kept going, which was a lot of talking for Viho, especially in the presence of so many witnesses. "I don't even care how we describe our relationship. I'd be proud to call you my fiancée or wife. But as long as you feel this connection as strongly as I do, that's all that matters. The more I get to know you, the more I realize that you do. And this…what you've put on your arm, for my mom…for *me*… Well, you've blown me away. Today and every day, Sterling. I'm in awe that I've found a woman like you to spend my life with. Whatever we call that."

She heard someone sniffle in the background and was afraid she might be joining them soon. Damn hormones.

"Getting her name tattooed on your ass might help your case here, buddy." Clayton couldn't help himself.

"No!" Sterling sat upright. "Don't mess with perfection."

Viho chuckled. "I do think my butt is my best

feature."

"It's not." She drew him to her for a kiss. "Your eyes are. And your giant heart. I'm sorry that I've trampled it a time or two. I promise I'll try to trod lighter in the future. I'm sure I'm going to screw up a time or four-thousand, but I hope you'll find some way to forgive me."

"I will. Because I know you don't mean it." He sighed. "I wasted so much time focusing on everything wrong with my life that I might have missed out on good stuff too. It's like when you start to see things through that negative lens, it all looks ugly. Since I've met you, you've helped me put things in perspective. Sure, things aren't always roses and sunshine, but it's how you cope that counts. Right?"

She nodded.

"Not to interrupt or anything," Wyatt said, completely interrupting.

Hope smacked him, but he kept on going. "My Compass Girl taught me that what was doesn't have to be what will be. I think that might be important for you to know too. Just because shit happened to you before, it doesn't mean it will again. Or that you have to deal with it the same way. You're older...*way older*...and wiser now."

Viho flashed the guy a friendly middle finger. Then he said, "So just one more thing, before we wrap up all this sentimental bullshit and get back to regularly scheduled life..."

"Yeah?" Sterling couldn't wait until they were alone and she could jump him. He was getting hotter by the second.

"I have something. I'm holding it for you. Refer back to the not-asking-you-to-marry-me thing. Okay? Promise?" He actually hesitated. After all the rest he'd said, this had to be a doozie.

"Sure." She hoped she could keep that oath.

"Guess it turns out that Jake wanted to marry my mom before she took off. And as much as I loved her, I'm starting to see a different side of things the more I get to know him. Anyway, he had this. For her. But he never got a chance to give it to her." From beneath his shirt, Viho withdrew an engagement ring.

It wasn't super flashy or even that unique when she appraised it with her jeweler's eye, but it was classy and perfect.

Absolutely flawless when she viewed it with her heart.

"Holy shit," Liam whisper-shouted.

"You're making us look bad over here, dude," Clayton grumbled, though he was immediately shushed by the other Compass Girls.

"And he gave it to you?" Sterling reached out a finger to trace the circle of the ring Jake had kept safe all these years. He'd never surrendered it, or his heart, to anyone else.

"To us." Viho smiled softly. "Along with his blessing. I guess he thinks I'm not such a delinquent after all. But I'm not giving it to you."

"You're really not?" Why was she suddenly plagued with disappointment?

"Nope." He shook his head. "I'm holding it for you. Waiting for the right moment. Whenever that may come. The day you're ready to accept it, all you have to do is say the word and it's yours. Until then, I'll keep it safe for you. Just like my father did for my mother."

"What if I'm never ready?" Sterling worried out loud.

"Oh my God, Sterling." Sienna smacked herself in the forehead. "You're having his baby. You're totally in love with the man. How much *readier* do you have to be?"

"It's okay," Viho reassured her. "I'll wait. And figure out how to be a better partner in the meantime. I have a lot of learning to do. It could take a while."

"As soon as I'm done with this tattoo…" Sterling began.

"You're finished, honey." The artist nudged her. "Put the man out of his misery, please."

"Right. Help me up?" She peeked at Viho. As if she weighed no more than the bubble mailers she packed her jewelry in, he scooped her from the chair.

Hard to say if the room was spinning from going upright so quickly, the momentous events of the day, or simply being around the guy who would be the core of her new family.

"Viho." Sterling would have sunk to her knees, but Viho didn't allow it. Instead he parked her on his lap, where he could cradle her against his heat and strength.

"Yes?" He smiled softly at her.

"This poor ring has waited long enough to be worn by someone who appreciates it. I love Jake and if I'd known your mom I know I would have adored her too. But part of me is furious at them for wasting what they had. For hurting you in the process. I don't want to make those same mistakes. I'm ready to put it on, to accept your promise and make vows of my own. I don't want to miss out like Jake and Haiwee. What a tragedy that would be. I was wrong. So wrong. There's nothing more to hold out for. You're the man I'm meant to be with. Forever. Will *you* marry *me*?"

Sighs and ahhs echoed around them.

Until he surprised them all.

"Not any time soon. Nope." He shrugged, and she knew what he was doing.

Not striking back at her, but ensuring she was certain. And she was. He made her more so with every exhibit he gave that he truly understood her.

"I meant it when I said the label doesn't matter. We're already living our life together. After we're settled, once the baby is born and our life is routine…boring missionary sex on Sunday mornings…"

"Gah, gross." Jade stuck out her tongue.

"Okay, maybe not that extreme." He laughed, and Sterling joined him. Then he clarified, "But once we're steady, then we'll make it official. And not before."

"For the record." Sterling tipped his chin down so she could stare into his eyes. "I *know* you're the one."

"I'm sure too." He stole a kiss, then continued, "And if we're both right, then it won't hurt anything to wait. It only changes things if we're wrong."

"Which you're not," Hope interjected.

"Right." Viho treated them all to that rare, blinding grin that illuminated her soul with light and love.

"You're the smartest man I know, Viho. And the handsomest." Sterling kissed him while the other Compass Girls and their guys contested her assessment.

"If she wasn't already pregnant, I'm pretty sure a kiss like that could have done the job." Jade kicked their chair. "Come on, lovebirds. Vivi's waiting. Now that we've done this, I can't wait to show her."

"She's going to love them." Sterling peeked at her arm before hugging the artist. "Thank you."

They pulled out their wallets to pay, but the manager refused to accept their cards. "It's on the house. You've given us enough by letting us be part of what happened here today. With those two… and with your grandmother. Vicky Compton petitioned for us to get our license when the rest of the town thought we were hoodlums. Without her, we wouldn't even be here."

"I'd forgotten about that." Jade grinned. "Way to go, Vivi."

"Tell her we say hello. And thank you."

The Compass Girls and their respective guys left in pairs, plus a trio, but they'd never be apart again, joined by their matching declarations of their heritage.

Compass Girls for life—by blood, and by choice.

Chapter Fourteen

Sterling couldn't stop staring at the modest round brilliant cut diamond on her finger as Viho drove them back to Compass Ranch. Well, it was a tossup between that and the colorful artwork decorating her arm, which peeked through her clear bandage, vying for her attention. They both meant so much to her, more than she could have expected a few short months ago.

"You know, you could reset the stone. I'm sure he wouldn't mind if you made it your own." Viho stopped just short of calling Jake "Dad". Still, he'd quit referring to him by his first name. It was progress. And in time, *Dad* would come naturally—she knew it would.

Sterling reached across to squeeze Viho's thigh.

He'd only been part of their lives for a quarter of a year, but a season was long enough to change a person's entire trajectory. Hell, a single moment could do the trick if it was the right one. At the right time. Lived in with the right person.

A memory of Viho, standing on the side of the road with his arms behind him on the bed of that rusty truck flashed into her memory, and she grinned. He'd been there, just waiting for her to pick him up.

"No, it's perfect like this." There was nothing she

would change. About the ring. Him. Their future.

They sloshed inside the Jeep as the vehicle pulled onto the gravel road leading into the heart of Compass Ranch where Vivi waited for them. She was the only thing Sterling wished she could change. The baby growing inside her would never know the woman who had done so much to shape Sterling's life, her beliefs, her personality.

Except through the endless stories they would share about her.

"Do you think...?" Sterling cut herself off.

"Hmm?" Viho glanced at her before returning his attention to the road. He reached over and held her hand. "What were you going to say?"

She swallowed.

"If the baby is a girl, do you think we could name her after Vicky?" Quickly she realized that might be selfish. "Or something for your mom. Maybe both?"

"Of course." The look he shot her was filled with gratitude and love. "What if I tell you the name of each of the flowers in my people's language? You could pick something you like."

"That's perfect." She blinked to clear the mist from her vision. "I want our child to learn your customs. Maybe you could teach me too?"

"You'd do that?" He peeked at her from the corner of his eyes.

"Yes. I want to know all of you. Understand your history."

"I'm more concerned about my future." He shrugged.

"Me too. But those things are part of who you are, and I love you because of them."

Viho didn't reply right away, but he toyed with the ring on her finger. "This is the smartest thing I've ever done."

"Well, technically, I did it for you." She giggled as they pulled up to the house. Before she could climb out herself, Viho had jogged around and opened her door. He plucked her from the car and spun her around in his arms a few times before letting her slide down his sculpted body, pausing only to steal a kiss before her toes touched the ground once more.

"Oh, come on already." Jade stood at the top of the porch stairs. "You can molest each other later. Everyone's here. And I can't wait anymore to show these bad boys off."

"All right, all right." Sterling took Viho's hand and raced up to join her cousins and the men who loved them. Together, they went inside, careful not to slam Vivi's screen door.

It did seem kind of crowded inside, like all of their relatives had showed up at once. She should have figured that their parents would be nosy and want to see their tattoos as soon as they were complete.

The four Compass Girls held hands as they walked toward Vivi's chair, linked.

But when they approached, they noticed Jake, standing behind it with one hand on her shoulder. Beyond them, the rest of the family milled around, none of them looking especially interested in the big reveal.

"What's going on?" Jade asked Jake.

"Vivi's taken a bit of a turn." He stopped before saying *a turn for the worse*, as Sterling expected. "Dr. Martin left a little while ago. He feels the change could be permanent."

Before they could draw more information from him, Vivi turned toward them and smiled. "Hello there, pretty girls. Aren't you a bunch of sweet ones?"

Stunned, Sterling didn't know what to do. Viho hugged her from behind, his hands over her belly. Each of the other Compass Girls stood similarly in shock.

Supported by their guys but reeling together.

This couldn't be! She had to see their tattoos. To know them and understand how much they loved her.

"It doesn't matter, Sterling," Viho whispered in her ear, "Your Vivi knew what she meant to you. The art is really for you, sweetheart."

Still, when Jade went to her knees on the floor before their grandmother, each of the Compass Girls followed suit with their guys standing tall behind them.

"What happened to your arm, dear?" Vivi asked Hope.

"It's a tattoo." The tears were evident in her voice.

"Did it hurt so much?" Vivi tipped her head. "I've always sort of fancied getting one myself. Ever since my boys got matching tattoos. Big, fancy things. Takes up most of their backs. They're great pieces art, showing their devotion to Compass Ranch and to their father, JD."

None of them dared interrupt when she seemed so happy. It hammered home to Sterling how proud and honored she would have been by their gesture.

"My cousins and I all got a similar design." Sienna gestured to the other ladies around her. "Would you like to see? They're kind of like your sons'. But ours are for a very special woman. Our grandmother. She loves flowers."

When Sienna got too choked up to continue, Jade took over pointing out the finer details they'd etched into themselves while their parents looked on from Jake's side of the chair. Though their smiles were watery, they clearly approved.

"What a coincidence!" Vivi clutched her hands to her chest. "I adore those too. I have a garden. My husband planted it for me. It's the most beautiful thing to sit there, surrounded by all the blooms. I especially love this."

She pointed to the magnolia at the center of the bunch that represented herself.

And not one of them could keep a dry eye.

"Those are fantastic, girls. The colors are so vibrant and lifelike. Except they'll never wilt." Vivi looked closely, engrossed. "You know, I'd love it if you'd stick around a bit. Would you join me and my husband, JD, for dinner? He would enjoy hearing your story and I'm sure he'll love your tattoos too. Pretty art for pretty girls."

Sterling looked up at Jake, who nodded, encouraging her to play along. "Sure, we'll stay."

"Terrific!" Vivi smiled so wide and bright, Sterling knew she'd never seen that much happiness radiating from her grandmother. And that was saying a lot. "He'll be home as soon as the evening chores are finished and the animals are taken care of. Wait until you meet him. He's a handsome devil and smart too. I'm the luckiest woman in Compton Pass."

Sterling couldn't stand it a moment longer. She bolted to her feet and ran into the kitchen, where Vivi couldn't witness her tears of disappointment.

Viho held her, rocking her as a sob broke free of her chest.

It wasn't long though before soft footfalls indicated someone joined them.

"Who are you crying for, Sterling?" Jake asked from across the kitchen. "If it's her, don't bother. She's finally happy again and will be until the disease claims her body as well as her mind. It's a blessing."

"How can you say that?" Sterling cried. Viho held her arm, steadying her as she rounded on his father.

"Look at her. She's radiant." He smiled softly and with more than a little envy in his gaze. "Finally, she doesn't remember being alone. She has JD back. The impossible has happened."

Sterling watched as Vivi rambled on about what they would have for dinner and how hard JD worked growing the ranch. She was filled with pride and excitement.

"It's time to let her go." Jake approached. He wrapped her in a hug. "It's selfish of us to keep her with us longer. I hope she never remembers. That she never suffers from that loss again."

For once, it seemed like Jake would get his wish.

It was then, as Sterling covered her face with her hands, that he noticed the flash of light on her finger.

"Well, look at that." He whooped as he took her hand in his.

"I think the news is out," Sienna said to Daniel as she plugged her ears.

And as if they had supernatural powers, Cindi and each of her aunts picked up on the excitement, swooping in for a closer look.

"It had been a while since we had a proper wedding around here. Now we're going to have a few in a row, huh?" Aunt Lucy smiled as she glanced around the room. "Never get tired of those."

"Does this mean we have to dress up again?" Bryant, Sterling's little brother, griped.

"Damn straight," Liam teased him. "If I have to wear a tux, so do you."

"Well, that may be true for the other girls, but we're planning to take our time." Sterling couldn't help the smile that returned to her face. "So we'll stretch out the partying."

Her mother didn't wait another instant to squeeze her in a hug while her father slapped Viho on the back. Then he looked to Jake, "It looks like you and I are officially going to be family after all."

Jake's eyes widened and then he grinned. "I suppose you're right. Woohoo!"

Meanwhile, Cindi rotated Sterling's hand this way and that, admiring the pretty stone. "Jake, this looks just like…"

"It is." He nodded. "Haiwee's ring."

Sterling's mom left her side then to hug Jake tight.

"Something Vicky said to me today rang true," he told her. "It's time for me to let go of the past and live the rest of my life without regrets. I'm looking forward to all these new beginnings."

"Did someone get engaged?" Vicky asked from the living room and Sterling was shuffled in to show off her rock once again. It didn't really get old. Even better was reintroducing Vivi to Viho, lavishing him with all of the love she held for him.

"This calls for a celebration." She smiled. "Who's going to help me make a cake to go with dinner? JD's favorite is chocolate, if you don't mind indulging me for his sake."

"That sounds great," Sterling said, and she realized it was true. Jake was right. This was how it should be. Spending time together, enjoying the last days they had in each other's company without fear, or pain, or anger.

And though Vivi really only supervised, each ingredient they added ensured her love was baked into the cake, which they would eat together as a family.

Of course the Compass Girls started a flour battle, which demolished the entire kitchen once their little brothers joined the fray and escalated the good-natured confrontation to a war.

Everyone pitched in after that, making a meal that they could share as they listened to Vivi tell stories of the olden days as if they were fresh and new. They learned things long forgotten by all as if they'd been there themselves.

And when the dishes piled high and pants buttons were unfastened to make more room, the cake was brought into the middle of the crowd. Viho chuckled as he plucked a glob of chocolate from Sterling's hair as they not-so-patiently waited for the treat to be sliced and handed around.

Before they took their first bites, though, Silas Compton stood from his place at the head of the table and addressed them all. Even the most rambunctious of the Compass Boys went still and quiet when he spoke.

"I want to say thank you to everyone gathered here today for making what could have been a terrible day one I will remember for the rest of my life and smile as I think back on it. So enjoy the dessert and good luck at getting seconds in this crowd. Together, let's celebrate lives lived fully. And pledge that each of us will carry on with that, the most important Compass family tradition of all."

"Let's eat!" yelled Sam.

And no more talking could be heard over the clink of forks on plates.

Epilogue

"Gramp Jake!" Lomasi squealed as she skipped to her most favorite person in the whole world. Except for Mommy and Daddy, of course. Gram Cin and Pop Sam too. Plus her cousins. All the lots and lots of them. "Imma flower girl!"

"Yes, you are, sweetheart." He laughed as he picked her up and twirled her around. "In many ways. Did you know that your pretty name means *good flower*?"

"Nope. What's that?"

"It's a blossom that's perfect and gorgeous. Like you. But if you're not careful, you're going to be a messy, dirt-covered flower girl before you've done your job. And then your mommy will be mad at me. Remember we talked about that?"

"Yep." She held out her hand and ticked off her fingers, like Gramp Jake and Mommy had done to her lots of times lately. "Gonna smile. Throw petals in the air. Not get dirty. And be quiet during the boooooooring parts."

"Right." Gramp Jake smiled down at her. "Not too much longer now until we get started. Then there will be dancing and music. You can get as messy as you want."

"Promise?"

"Yup." He laughed. "Guess what?"

She perked up, since that always meant something fun. "Hmm?

"There's even going to be a cake. The biggest one you've ever seen." He waggled his eyebrows, making her laugh.

"Chocolate or vanilla?" Lomasi tapped her chin, not sure which she liked better.

"Both."

"Yippee!" This really was the best day ever. "Can we eat some now?"

"No, only after you do your flower girling. Here, let me show you some of the nicest flowers in Vivi's garden, okay?" It was a distraction, but she didn't mind.

"Uh-huh. Did Daddy really plant these all by himself?" She tickled a floppy purple petal. It dropped off and fell in her basket like the oodles of others she'd collected.

"He did." Gramp Jake swooped her up and carried her, not letting her squish her shiny shoes in the muddy patch she'd been aiming for.

"So why they call it Vivi's garden?" She tipped her head and clung to Gramp Jake's neck, so high above the ground. Almost as tall as when Daddy carried her. "It should be Daddy Garden."

"It's named after a special lady."

"Is she coming to the wedding?" Lomasi sure would like to meet her if she got *all* the flowers named after her.

"No, baby." Gramp Jake sighed, making her go up and down on his chest.

"Why not?" She pouted, sticking her lower lip out like she did when she wanted candy. Sometimes her daddy got meanie and made her eat stinky vegetables first, but the lip usually worked.

"She's in heaven." Gramp Jake took a red flower, the one they called rose, she thought, and poked it into her hair so it stuck. She patted it, liking how it felt.

"With Gram Haiwee." She nodded. "Maybe they're having their own party and wearing pretty, no-dirts-allowed dresses together. Fancy hats too. And long white gloves."

Mommy had a black-and-white picture like that of a lady on top of the fireplace.

"You know, I bet they are. They would be very happy today." Gramp Jake stopped talking for a while. He rubbed his eye like it had something in it.

Then he hugged her so tight he kind of squished her, but she didn't complain.

"Here." Gramp Jake set her down, then took her to a bench beneath the big tree. At the bottom of it was a square stone with squiggly lines and a picture. "This is Vivi and her husband, JD."

"He looks at her like Daddy looks at Mommy." She tapped the nice man on the head.

"You're right, he does."

For a little bit, they were quiet as she studied the nice man and lady. Until she spotted her daddy crossing the lawn in funny black clothes. "Daddy!"

She squirmed until Gramp Jake let go of her hand so she could meet Daddy, loving the way her skirt flounced as she skipped.

"Hi, Peanut." He planted lots of extra-loud kisses on her cheeks as she squealed. "You look so pretty. How'd you get out here?"

"I was bored," she shrugged. "They're taking too long. So I came outside to play with Gramp Jake."

"Smart girl," her Uncle Bryant said. She hadn't seen him and his boyfriend following behind Daddy, but once she noticed them she stuck out her arms so they could hold her too. They were nice. And funny.

And looked at each other like the people in the Vivi picture. She liked hopping from person to person, getting lots of hugs.

It seemed like there was never a time when there weren't lots of people around to give her some. When the novelty wore off, she skipped around Daddy's long legs.

"When will Mommy be ready?" She twirled the basket, watching all the colorful petals zoom around inside.

"Probably by midnight," her cousin Austin said, all grumpy.

"That long?" Her bottom lip wobbled as she felt like she might cry. "But that's after my bedtime. I'm supposed to throw flowers."

"Sorry, kiddo." He picked her up and wooshed her around, making her laugh. "I was only teasing. Girls go crazy over all this wedding stuff. It's so fancy schmancy."

"Not Mommy." Lomasi would have crossed her arms if she could have. "She didn't even get the princess dress that I liked best."

"No?" Daddy squatted down and traced one of the ringlets dangling by her face. "I'm not surprised. She's not that kind of girl. I know she's beautiful, though, whatever she's wearing."

"Well, when *I* get married, I'm going to have the biggest, poofiest, *sparkliest* dress ever. And a tiara. And I'ma ride a unicorn." She twirled around for effect.

"Good to know, baby. I'll start saving now." Daddy groaned and his best mens—Uncle Wyatt and Uncle Clayton—laughed, slapping him on the back.

"Enjoy while you can, guys." He grinned at them. "You could be in the same boat soon enough, now that you knocked Hope up. Maybe even double, since she's having twins."

"What's that mean?" Lomasi's ears perked up.

"Uh, nothing." Daddy cursed under his breath. "Pretend you didn't hear that."

"Or the bad word you just said?"

"Yep, that too." He shook his head. "Hey, I see you've got Mr. Turtle."

"Uh huh." She nodded. "Mommy made him into this necklace for me so that I don't lose him and I can take him with me wherever I go from now on."

"I bet he'll like that." Daddy smiled down at her. "I'm glad you have him today."

"He didn't want to miss the wedding." Lomasi told him. "He's the flower turtle, you know?"

"Uh, okay." He sounded like he wasn't paying attention anymore.

So she looked up to see what he was doing. And found him staring across the lawn to the main house where her mommy had just come outside. Finally.

"We'd better go get in place." Gramp Jake took her hand and stood near the back while Daddy kissed her, then went to the front like they practiced. Except this time he was sniffling like he had a cold.

"What's wrong with Daddy?" she asked Gramp Jake.

"Nothing, baby," he promised. "He's happy, that's all."

"Okie dokie." Lomasi waited super extra quiet while everyone turned to look in their direction. But not at her. They stood as her cousins Sienna, Hope and Jade walked past with Daniel, Liam, Wyatt and Clayton. She wished she could play with them.

They were all more of her favorite people, even though they looked so different today with the purple dresses they wore instead of their jeans and T-shirts.

Pretty soon a lady with a violin played a song and everyone stood up.

"Okay, it's your turn." Gramp Jake set her on the end of the aisle so she could dance between the chairs and throw the petals everywhere. Maybe they'd said walk, but she felt like dancing. People clapped and giggled and took her picture, and soon she'd made it through with Gramp Jake scooping her up on the other end.

He held her as her mommy walked down the aisle with Pop Sam holding her arm. And Lomasi thought maybe her mommy had been right. That was the prettiest dress ever.

Although there were some boring parts, it was worth it once everyone cheered and they made their way to one of the barns on the ranch for the party. Fairy lights and lots of flowers had been strung up everywhere inside. She wished it could look like this every day, but then it wouldn't be special.

Or at least that's what Mommy told her when she asked if they could stay.

After lots of eating, and drinking and dancing and more eating of the yummy cake, Lomasi curled up on the blanket Gramp Jake had laid over a comfy pile of hay. The hanging lights sparkled in her eyes as they grew blurry.

The music and people dancing lulled the newest Compton to sleep, secure in the love of a vast and ever-growing family. Though some had gone before and others would leave after, there would always be people to take their places and keep Compton Pass, Wyoming alive in the hearts and spirits of all who'd been lucky enough to call it home.

What Happens Next?

If you've enjoyed the Compass Brothers and the Compass Girls, make sure you keep your eyes peeled for four more books in the Compass universe. Yes, that's right. Everyone's favorite little brothers are getting their stories soon!

About the Authors

Jayne Rylon and Mari Carr met at a writing conference in June 2009 and instantly became arch enemies. Two authors couldn't be more opposite. Mari, when free of her librarian-by-day alter ego, enjoys a drink or two or... more. Jayne, allergic to alcohol, lost huge sections her financial-analyst mind to an epic explosion resulting from Mari gloating about her hatred of math. To top it off, they both had works in progress with similar titles and their heroes shared a name. One of them would have to go.

The battle between them for dominance was a bloody, but short one, when they realized they'd be better off combining their forces for good (or smut). With the ink dry on the peace treaty, they emerged as good friends, who have a remarkable amount in common despite their differences, and their writing partnership has flourished. Except for the time Mari attempted to poison Jayne with a bottle of Patron. Accident or retaliation? You decide.

Join Mari's newsletter and Jayne's Naughty News so you don't miss new releases, contests, or exclusive subscriber-only content.

Jayne Rylon and Mari Carr

Also by Jayne Rylon

MEN IN BLUE
Hot Cops Save Women In Danger
Night is Darkest
Razor's Edge
Mistress's Master
Spread Your Wings
Wounded Hearts
Bound For You

DIVEMASTERS
Sexy SCUBA Instructors By Day, Doms On A Mega-Yacht By Night
Going Down
Going Deep
Going Hard

POWERTOOLS
Five Guys Who Get It On With Each Other & One Girl. Enough Said?
Kate's Crew
Morgan's Surprise
Kayla's Gift
Devon's Pair
Nailed to the Wall
Hammer it Home

HOT RODS
Powertools Spin Off. Keep up with the Crew plus...
Seven Guys & One Girl. Enough Said?
King Cobra

Mustang Sally
Super Nova
Rebel on the Run
Swinger Style
Barracuda's Heart
Touch of Amber
Long Time Coming

STANDALONE
Menage
4-Ever Theirs
Nice & Naughty
Contemporary
Where There's Smoke
Report For Booty

COMPASS BROTHERS
Modern Western Family Drama Plus Lots Of Steamy Sex
Northern Exposure
Southern Comfort
Eastern Ambitions
Western Ties

COMPASS GIRLS
Daughters Of The Compass Brothers Drive Their Dads Crazy And Fall In Love
Winter's Thaw
Hope Springs
Summer Fling
Falling Softly

PLAY DOCTOR
Naughty Sexual Psychology Experiments Anyone?
Dream Machine

Healing Touch

RED LIGHT
A Hooker Who Loves Her Job
Complete Red Light Series Boxset
FREE - Through My Window - FREE
Star
Can't Buy Love
Free For All

PICK YOUR PLEASURES
Choose Your Own Adventure Romances!
Pick Your Pleasure
Pick Your Pleasure 2

RACING FOR LOVE
MMF Menages With Race-Car Driver Heroes
Complete Series Boxset
Driven
Shifting Gears

PARANORMALS
Vampires, Witches, And A Man Trapped In A Painting
Paranormal Double Pack Boxset
Picture Perfect
Reborn

Look for these titles by Mari Carr

Falling Softly

Big Easy
Blank Canvas
Crash Point
Full Position
Rough Draft
Triple Beat
Winner Takes All
Going Too Fast

Boys of Fall:
Free Agent
Red Zone
Wild Card

Compass:
Northern Exposure
Southern Comfort
Eastern Ambitions
Western Ties
Winter's Thaw
Hope Springs
Summer Fling
Falling Softly

Farepoint Creek:
Outback Princess
Outback Cowboy
Outback Master
Outback Lovers

June Girls:
No Recourse
No Regrets

Just Because:
Because of You
Because You Love Me
Because It's True

Lowell High:
Bound by the Past
Covert Affairs
Mad about Meg

Bundles
Cowboy Heat
Sugar and Spice
Madison Girls
Scoundrels

Second Chances:
Fix You
Dare You
Just You
Near You
Reach You
Always You

Sparks in Texas:
Sparks Fly
Waiting for You
Something Sparked
Off Limits
No Other Way
Whiskey Eyes

Trinity Masters:
Elemental Pleasure
Primal Passion
Scorching Desire
Forbidden Legacy
Hidden Devotion
Elegant Seduction
Secret Scandal
Delicate Ties

Wild Irish:
Come Monday
Ruby Tuesday
Waiting for Wednesday
Sweet Thursday
Friday I'm in Love
Saturday Night Special
Any Given Sunday
Wild Irish Christmas
January Girl
February Stars

Individual Titles:
Seducing the Boss
Tequila Truth
Erotic Research
Rough Cut
Happy Hour
Power Play
One Daring Night
Assume the Positions
Slam Dunk

What Was Your Favorite Part?

Did you enjoy this book? If so, please leave a review and tell your friends about it. Word of mouth and online reviews are immensely helpful and greatly appreciated.

Jayne's Shop

Check out Jayne's online shop for autographed print books, direct download ebooks, reading-themed apparel up to size 5XL, mugs, tote bags, notebooks, Mr. Rylon's wood (you'll have to see it for yourself!) and more.

www.jaynerylon.com/shop

Listen Up!

The majority of Jayne's books are also available in audio format on Audible, Amazon and iTunes.

Printed in Great Britain
by Amazon